Praise for Marta Perry

"Terrific family story, touching throughout…
Kudos to Marta Perry for such an inspiring novel."
—*RT Book Reviews* on *Mission: Motherhood*

"Marta Perry writes a warm, loving story…"
—*RT Book Reviews* on *A Soldier's Heart*

"Marta Perry is synonymous with sweet, loving
romance!"
—*RT Book Reviews* on *A Father's Place*

Praise for Jo Ann Brown

"The story is rich with relatable struggles and
characters."
—*RT Book Reviews* on *Amish Homecoming*

"An engrossing story."
—*RT Book Reviews* on *A Hero for Christmas*

"Brown's latest is a sweet tale of the transformative
power of love."
—*RT Book Reviews* on *Promise of a Family*

A lifetime spent in rural Pennsylvania and her Pennsylvania Dutch heritage led **Marta Perry** to write about the Plain People who add so much richness to her home state. Marta has seen nearly sixty of her books published, with over six million books in print. She and her husband live in a centuries-old farmhouse in a central Pennsylvania valley. When she's not writing, she's reading, traveling, baking or enjoying her six beautiful grandchildren.

Jo Ann Brown has always loved stories with happy-ever-after endings. A former military officer, she is thrilled to have the chance to write stories about people falling in love. She is also a photographer, and she travels with her husband of more than thirty years to places where she can snap pictures. They live in Nevada with three children and a spoiled cat. Drop her a note at joannbrownbooks.com.

Amish Christmas Blessings

Marta Perry

&

Jo Ann Brown

 LOVE INSPIRED BOOKS

ISBN-13: 978-0-373-71988-4

Amish Christmas Blessings

Copyright © 2016 by Harlequin Books S.A.

The publisher acknowledges the copyright holders of the individual works as follows:

The Midwife's Christmas Surprise
Copyright © 2016 by Martha Johnson

A Christmas to Remember
Copyright © 2016 by Jo Ann Ferguson

www.Harlequin.com

Printed in U.S.A.

CONTENTS

THE MIDWIFE'S
CHRISTMAS SURPRISE

Marta Perry

This story is dedicated to my husband, Brian, with much love.

If anyone has caused grief, he has not so much grieved me as he has grieved all of you...

—*2 Corinthians* 2:5

Chapter One

If the door to the exam room at the birthing center hadn't been ajar, Anna Zook would never have heard the hurtful comment.

"...so long as you're the one to catch the baby, and not the Zook girl. She's too young and inexperienced to be birthing my first grandchild."

The door closed abruptly, cutting off anything else that might be said, but Anna recognized the speaker— Etta Beachy, mother-in-law of one of her partner Elizabeth's clients. Despite the fact that Anna had been a full partner in the midwife practice for over a year, many in Lost Creek's Amish community still saw her as the quiet, shy girl she'd been when she began her apprenticeship with Elizabeth.

The December chill outside seemed to seep into her heart. Would the people of Lost Creek ever accept her as midwife, or would she always be walking in Elizabeth's shadow?

Anna tried to concentrate on the patient record she was reviewing, but the doubts kept slipping between her and the page. It was natural enough that folks turned to Elizabeth, she told herself firmly. Elizabeth Miller had been the only midwife in the isolated northern Pennsylvania Amish settlement for over twenty years. It would just take time and patience for them to accept her, wouldn't it?

The door opened, and a little parade came out—Etta Beachy, looking as if she'd just bit into a sour pickle, her daughter-in-law, Dora, who looked barely old enough for marriage, let alone motherhood, and Elizabeth, whose round, cheerful face was as serene as always.

Small wonder folks trusted Elizabeth—she radiated a sense of calm and assurance that was instantly soothing. Much as Anna tried to model herself on Elizabeth, she never quite succeeded in doing that.

A blast of cold air came into the outer office as the front door opened, and Anna spotted young James leap down from the buggy seat, clutching a blanket to wrap around his wife.

Elizabeth closed the door behind them and turned to Anna, rubbing her arms briskly. "Brr. It's cold enough to snow, but Asa says not yet."

Anna nodded, knowing Elizabeth, so confident in her own field, trusted her husband implicitly when it came to anything involving the farm. Maybe that was the secret of their strong marriage—the confidence each had in the other.

"You heard what Etta said, ain't so?" Elizabeth's keen gaze probed for any sign that Anna was upset.

"Ach, it's nothing I haven't heard before." Anna

managed to smile. "Naturally Etta feels that way. She's known you all her life."

"Then she ought to trust my judgment in training you." Elizabeth sounded as tart as she ever did. "I think Dora might be happier with you, being closer to her age and all, but she's too shy to venture an opinion different from Etta's."

"It will all be forgotten when they see the baby. When are you thinking it will be?"

"Most likely not until well after Christmas." As if the words had unleashed something, Elizabeth's blue eyes seemed to darken with pain. She glanced out the side window toward the farmhouse, making Anna wonder what she saw there other than the comfortable old farmhouse that had sheltered generations of the Miller family.

"Elizabeth?" Anna stood, moving quickly to put her arm around her friend's waist. "What is it?"

"Ach, nothing. Just foolishness." Elizabeth shook her head, but she couldn't disguise the tears in her eyes.

"Tell me," Anna said gently, longing to help.

The older woman brushed a tear away impatiently. "Nothing." She bit her lip. "It's just…this will be the third Christmas without Benjamin."

The name struck Anna like a blow to the heart. She forced herself to concentrate on Elizabeth's pain, not allowing herself to recognize her own. "I know," she murmured. "Perhaps…" Anna tried to think of something reassuring to say, but what was there?

Benjamin, Elizabeth and Asa's third son, had walked

away from the Amish faith and his family three years ago. And her. He'd walked away from her, as well.

"I'm sorry," she said finally, knowing how inadequate it was. Elizabeth didn't know there'd ever been anything between her son and her young apprentice, and that was probably for the best, given how things had turned out.

Elizabeth sucked in a breath and straightened. "Asa doesn't want to talk about Ben's leaving. I try not to burden him with my sorrow. But oh, if only our boy would come home to us."

"Maybe he will." Did she wish that? For Elizabeth's happiness, for sure. But for herself—how would she manage if Benjamin did come back?

"I keep praying. That's all I can do." Elizabeth pressed her cheek against Anna's for a moment. "Ach, I must get back to the house and start some supper. Are you coming now?"

Anna shook her head. "I'll finish cleaning up here first."

She'd lived with the Miller family since she'd come from Lancaster County as apprentice to Elizabeth. Each time she'd suggested she might find a place of her own, it had led to such an outcry that she'd given up, knowing Asa and Elizabeth meant it. They treated her as the daughter they'd given up on having after their four boys. How could she walk away from that?

Once Elizabeth had gone, Anna moved slowly around the four-room center, built by Asa and his sons so that Elizabeth would have a place close to home for meeting patients. Still, many of their mothers preferred having babies at home, so the two of them spent hours each week traveling from one Amish home to another.

When she found herself rearranging the stack of towels in the cabinet for the third time, Anna forced herself to recognize the truth. She was avoiding the thing she didn't want to think about—the beautiful, painful truth of her relationship with Benjamin.

Anna stood at the window, but she wasn't seeing the frigid winter landscape. Instead she looked up into the branches of the apple tree in the side yard, feeling the soft breeze of a summer evening brush her skin.

She and Benjamin had come home from a family picnic at the home of Ben's grandparents, and they'd loitered outside for a few minutes, watching the fireflies rise from the hay field and dance along the stream.

Ben had been telling her a story of climbing to the very top of the apple tree in response to a dare from one of his brothers. He'd fallen when a branch broke and broken his arm, but he didn't seem to regret it, laughing at the memory. That was Ben, always up for a dare.

She'd shifted her gaze from the branches to his laughing face, meaning to chide him for such foolishness, but her gaze became entangled with his, and her breath caught, the words dying.

Ben's eyes, blue as a summer sky, seemed to darken as he studied her face. His gaze had lingered on her lips. And then his lips had found hers, and a totally unexpected joy exploded inside her.

She'd never known how long they'd stood there, exchanging kisses, laughing that it had taken them so long to recognize the feelings between them, talking about a wedding. When she'd finally slipped into the house and up to her room, she'd held the warm assurance of his love close against her.

And the next day he'd been gone, leaving only a note for his parents saying he was going to see something of the world.

Anna tried to shake off the memories. She seldom let herself relive them, because the aftermath had seemed so painful. No one knew about her and Ben, so she'd had to pretend that her pain was only for Ben's family, not for herself.

After three years, it should have become easier. One night—that was all she had to block from her memories.

A final check around the center, and she was ready to go. She was just slipping on her coat when she heard a car pull up by the front door.

Anna frowned. One of their Englisch clients? No one was scheduled to come in today. She could only hope it wasn't an emergency.

Footsteps sounded on the porch, and she hurried to the door. She flung it open almost as soon as the knock sounded and stumbled back a step, the familiar room spinning around her.

The man standing on the porch wore boots, jeans and a black leather jacket zipped up against the cold, but he wasn't an Englischer. He was Benjamin Miller.

Of all the ways Ben had thought about his home-coming, the one he hadn't pictured was coming face to face with Anna Zook. She'd changed—that was his first automatic thought. He'd left behind a tender girl whose face had glowed with the impact of first love. Now he faced a woman who wore her maturity like a cloak around her.

"Anna." He said her name heavily, embarrassment and sorrow mixing in his tone. He didn't doubt he'd hurt her when he'd left. She had plenty of reasons not to welcome his return. "It's been a long time."

The words seemed to jolt her out of a daze. "Three years," she said tartly. "None of us have forgotten."

She seemed already armed against his return. Maybe that would make things easier. Whatever else happened here in Lost Creek, he couldn't hurt Anna again.

"I guess not." He gestured toward the door. "Mind if I come in?"

For an instant he thought she would slam it in his face. Then she nodded and stepped back, standing silent as he entered.

He looked around with appreciation. "The birthing center wasn't finished yet when I left. It looks good."

"Your father and brothers did fine work on building it just as your *mamm* wanted."

Was that a reminder that he hadn't been here to help? Probably so. He turned slowly to face her, letting his gaze drift over her. The honey-brown hair seemed to have lost its glints of gold, but maybe that was because it was December, not August. He'd always picture her under the apple tree on a summer night, her heart-shaped face tilted toward his, her green eyes lit with love.

"You've changed." It was inadequate, but it was the only thing he could think to say.

"People do in three years." She glanced at his leather jacket and jeans. "You have."

She couldn't know how much. If Anna's face showed her added maturity and assurance, his must be a map of disappointment and betrayal.

Time to leave behind this fruitless conversation and move on to the family. "Is Mamm at the house?"

Anna nodded, warily it seemed. "She went over a few minutes ago. We've finished with the patients for today, unless there's an emergency."

"I guess I'd best go and face the music, ain't so?" The familiar Pennsylvania Dutch phrase fell easily from his lips after training himself not to use it. He half turned toward the door and found that his feet didn't want to move. *Coward*, he told himself.

Still, his gaze sought Anna's face again. "My family—is everyone well?"

"So far as I know." She bit her lower lip, as if she'd like to say something else but restrained herself.

"If you're ready to go, I'll walk over with you."

She hesitated, and Ben recognized her reluctance. He opened the door, waiting, and Anna walked out with him.

The farm he'd grown up on spread out before him, the grass turning brown with winter's cold, the fruit trees bare. Resting, Daad would have said. Everything rested in winter, building up strength for the spring.

Funny. He'd never expected to cherish the most common of sights—the spring wagon parked beside the red barn, the windmill spinning in the strong breeze, the chickens pecking at the earth inside their pen, hunting for a forgotten bit of grain.

He'd left because he'd thought he didn't belong here. He'd learned the hard way he didn't belong in the outside world, either.

Could he come home again? They'd reached the back door that led into the kitchen. He was about to find out.

Anna hesitated on the step. "Maybe I should wait. Give you time with the family…"

"Mamm always said you were part of the family. There's no reason I can see to back off now." He may as well face all the people he'd disappointed at the same time. He seized the doorknob, turned it and stepped inside.

Daad and Joshua were sitting at the table. Mamm stood at the stove. All three of them turned to stare, seeming immobilized with shock. He waited, all the words he'd rehearsed deserting him.

Daad recovered first. He set down his coffee mug with a thud, his keen blue eyes fastened on Ben's face. Daad looked much the same—lean and wiry, his skin weathered from working outside. His beard was a little longer, a little grayer, that was all.

"So," he said. "You've come back."

It wasn't exactly the welcome given to the prodigal son, but he guessed it would have to do. "Ya," he said. "If you'll have me."

Daad's face was impassive. "It's your home."

As if he'd been waiting for Daad's reaction, Joshua scrambled to his feet, grinning. "It's *gut* to see you, Ben."

"Can this be my little *bruder*?" Ben grabbed his shoulder. "You're near as big as I am."

"What do you mean, near as big? I am as tall, ain't so?" Joshua, the youngest, had always been eager to catch up with his brothers.

"Maybe so." He was already looking beyond Josh to where his *mamm* stood, her hands twisting her apron.

The pain in her eyes shook him, and his heart wrenched. His throat grew tight. "Forgive me, Mammi," he murmured.

Tears filled her eyes, but to his relief they were tears of joy, not sorrow. She held her arms wide. "My Benjamin. You've *komm* home to us."

Ben stepped into her embrace, his heart overflowing with mingled grief and happiness. Grief for the pain he'd caused her—happiness at feeling her forgiveness wash over him in a healing flow.

If he could truly mend anywhere, it would be here. Mamm, at least, welcomed him with all her heart, despite the pain he'd caused.

Still holding her, he looked over her shoulder at the others. Josh, too young and too openhearted to hold a grudge, was still grinning. Daad—well, Daad was going to be more difficult. He was reserving his opinion, Ben thought. Not quite ready to go back to normal with the son who'd disappointed him so badly.

Anna stood with her back to the door. Anna had plenty of reason not to trust him. And right now she looked as if she thought welcoming him home was the worst idea in the world.

Chapter Two

It seemed to Anna that Elizabeth hadn't stopped smiling in the past twenty-four hours. She'd always known how much Elizabeth missed Benjamin and longed for his return, but she hadn't even realized how much that was reflected in her face. Elizabeth looked as if she'd shed ten years in a single day.

Anna led the buggy horse to the gate and then turned him into the field. Buck seemed to shrug all over, as if delighted to be rid of the harness. He sniffed the icy grass and then broke into a gallop, racing to where the other horses stood at the far end of the field.

Smiling at his antics, Anna headed for the house. She'd volunteered to take the home visits today, so that Elizabeth could be free to enjoy Benjamin's return.

But Anna couldn't deny that she'd had another motive, too. She'd been just as eager to get herself well away from Benjamin's disturbing presence.

Her steps slowed. She'd thought having time alone during the drive would give her a chance to come to terms with Benjamin's return. Unfortunately her thoughts just kept spinning around and around like the windmill blades in a strong wind.

Enough, she told herself. Was she reluctant to accept his return because she worried that he'd hurt his family again? Or was her concern more selfish?

When Anna put it to herself that way, she couldn't help but see the answer. Christians were called to forgiveness. They could only be forgiven as they forgave. If the rest of Benjamin's family could forgive him and welcome him back, then she must, too.

Holding on to the resolution firmly, she marched into the house. As always at this time of day, Elizabeth was in the kitchen. She was bent over the propane oven, her face flushed as she pulled out two apple pies, their crusts golden brown and the apple juices bubbling up through the vents.

"That wouldn't be Benjamin's favorite pie, would it?" Anna forced warmth into her voice as she stowed her medical bag on its shelf by the door.

"Ach, you caught me." Elizabeth transferred the pies to the wire cooling rack and turned, smiling.

Anna's heart gave a little thump. Elizabeth was so happy. How could Anna be skeptical of anything that made her feel that way?

"He'll appreciate those, I know." Surely nothing he'd found in the outside world could match his own *mamm*'s cooking. "Can I do anything?"

Elizabeth surveyed the pots on the stove top. "I don't think so." She glanced toward the clock. "Ben went out to cut some greens for me. I felt like getting ready for Christmas today. Maybe you'd go out and help him bring them to the porch. It'll soon be time for supper."

Well, she'd offered to help. Elizabeth wasn't to know that helping Ben…seeing Ben…was the last thing she wanted at the moment. All Anna could do was smile.

"Right away. Do you know where he went?" The woods began across the field behind the barn and stretched up to the ridge that sheltered the valley.

"That stand of hemlocks, I think. He knows I like the little cones on the greens to put on the windowsills."

Nodding, Anna buttoned her coat again and went back out into the cold. The brittle grass crackled under her shoes as she walked, and she scanned the skies for signs of snow. But the only clouds were light, wispy ones moving lazily across the blue.

It might be silly for a grown woman to be longing for that first snow of the winter, but she couldn't seem to help it. She loved running outside to feel the flakes melting on her face. She and her sisters used to vie to see who'd be first to catch a snowflake on her tongue.

A glimpse of black jacket among the hemlocks told her where Benjamin was, and she veered in his direction. Maybe it would be natural to wave or call out, but nothing felt natural when it came to Ben. Just the slightest glance from his deep blue eyes seemed to turn her back into the girl who'd thought she'd soon be a bride.

He had his back turned to her. The wheelbarrow next to him was full of green branches, and the clippers he'd been using lay atop them. Maybe he'd spotted a deer or a pheasant and was watching it, standing so still.

The clothes he wore were Amish, the black jacket a bit snug over his broad shoulders. Had he grown since he'd been gone? He certainly seemed taller and broader to her. The black pants and heavy shoes made her wonder what had become of the jeans and leather jacket. He wouldn't need them if he meant to be home for good.

Well, of course he'd come home to stay. He wouldn't be so unkind as to let his family believe that if it weren't so, would he?

His voice startled her. For a moment she thought he'd spoken to her, and then she realized he stood immobile because he was talking on a cell phone. Not so surprising, but still…

Don't judge. She had a cell phone herself, as well as the phone in the center. It was difficult to be a midwife to a widespread practice without one. She didn't use the phone casually, marking off for herself the line between what was accepted and what was bending the rules.

Ben might have a difficult time adjusting to living under the *Ordnung* again after his time out in the world. They'd all have to make allowances for him.

"That's not true." Ben's voice, raised in what might have been anger, came clearly to her ears. "Whatever happened between us is over."

Anna froze. She shouldn't be overhearing this. But she'd already heard. Should she make her presence known or attempt to creep silently backward?

"All right." Ben snapped the words. "I'll see you again, but not until I'm ready."

Anna took a step back, and a branch snapped beneath her foot, loud in the still air. Ben spun. His glare nailed her to the spot. She'd seen his eyes merry and laughing and teasing. And tender, filled with longing. But she'd never seen them freeze over with anger.

He clicked the phone off. "Eavesdropping, Anna?" The words were edged with ice.

Heat rushed to her cheeks. "Your mother sent me out to help you. I didn't realize what you were doing until…"

Her defense withered under his cold stare. When had he gotten those lines around his eyes, that tenseness in his jaw? That was new. Was that what the outside world had done to him?

"It didn't occur to you to let me know you were here, *ja*?" He bent to pick up the wheelbarrow handles. "You've done your duty. I'm coming. Why don't you run back and tell my *daad* that I was out here talking on my cell phone?"

A wave of anger came to her rescue. "I'm not a child, and I don't tattle on people."

"No." His gaze drifted over her. "I can see you're not a child, Anna. You're all grown up now."

Her anger edged up a notch at the way he'd looked at her. "Your clothes don't make you Amish, Benjamin. If you're not ready to leave the Englisch world, maybe you shouldn't have *komm*."

If anything, his face got tighter, until he didn't look remotely like the boy she'd loved. "Mamm may say you're like a daughter to her, but you're not family. It's not your business, so leave it alone."

Shoving the wheelbarrow, he strode off toward the house.

Anna stood where she was, fists clenched. So much for her resolutions. Maybe she could forgive Benjamin for what he'd done in the past. But what about what he planned to do in the future? How could she ever trust him again?

Ben walked into the kitchen after supper, intent on a last cup of coffee. The quick cadences of Pennsylvania Dutch came from the living room, where everyone was settled for the evening, Daad reading aloud something from the latest issue of the Amish newspaper, Mamm sewing and Josh whittling a tiny boat destined for their brother Daniel's oldest for Christmas. He hadn't realized how much he'd missed the sound of his native tongue, and it soothed his soul.

But he was leaving out someone. Anna was there as well, her lap filled with the baby shawl she was crocheting for Daniel and Barbie's youngest. When he'd said she wasn't part of the family, he'd wanted only to hurt her. Not only had that been unkind, it hadn't been true. Maybe she was more a member of the family than he was.

Standing at the counter, he stirred sugar into the coffee, his spoon clinking against the thick white mug. Mamm had already lined the kitchen windowsill with the greens he'd brought in. Amish might not have the Christmas trees that were everywhere in the outside world, but that didn't mean they didn't celebrate the season of Christ's birth in their own way.

A light step sounded behind him, and Ben knew without turning that it was Anna. Funny, how his view of her had changed. He'd thought her a quiet little mouse of a girl when she'd first come to stay with them. But he'd learned she had considerable spirit behind that quiet exterior. Today she'd turned it against him in reminding him that clothes didn't make him Amish, and he didn't like it.

"Ben." Her voice was soft. "May I speak with you for a moment?"

He turned. If she intended to reiterate her opinion of him...

Anna's heart-shaped face was serious, and a couple of lines had formed between her eyebrows. "I want to apologize." She seemed to have trouble getting the words out. "I had no right to speak to you the way I did. I'm sorry."

She'd disarmed him, taking away all the things he'd stored up to say.

"It's okay. I know you're just concerned about Mamm."

Some emotion he couldn't identify crossed her face, darkening her eyes. "She's not my mother, but I do care about her."

"I know." His voice roughened despite his effort at control. "Believe me, I don't want to hurt her."

He already had, hadn't he? Ben backed away from that thought.

"Gut." Anna hesitated. "I hope you're home to stay. It would mean so much to your family."

Would it mean anything to you, Anna? He shoved that thought away, not sure where it had come from.

"A lot has changed since I've been gone. I can't believe how Josh has grown. And think of Daniel and Barbie, having two *kinder* already. And I suppose Joseph will be next."

That brought a smile to her face, warming her eyes and showing him the beauty other people didn't seem to see. "I've never seen your *mamm* so nervous as when Barbie's little ones were born. She said I had to catch them because she couldn't, but believe me, she watched every move."

Ben leaned against the counter, cradling the mug in his hands as he studied her face. "So you're a partner now, not an apprentice. That's great."

Anna wrinkled her nose. "Now if we could just convince our clients of that…"

"Not willing to admit you're all grown up, are they? Folks are slow to move forward here, ain't so?"

She nodded, and again he saw that flicker of some emotion saddening her eyes. Did it worry her that people might still favor Mamm to deliver their babies?

They'd be wrong to discount Anna. There was a lot more to her than most folks thought, he'd guess. For an instant he saw her face turned up to his in the moonlight, alive with joy. Did no one else see that in her?

"Why aren't you married yet, Anna?" The question was out before he realized that it would be better not spoken. Talk about butting in where he didn't belong. "Sorry, I shouldn't…"

Daad came into the kitchen, interrupting the difficult moment. He glanced from Anna to him and then moved toward the coats hanging by the back door.

"I'm going out to check the stock. *Komm* with me, Ben?"

"Sure." Daad was getting him out of a difficult moment—that was certain sure.

Grabbing the black wool jacket that Mamm had put away in mothballs for his return, he followed Daad out the back door.

The air was crisp and cold, making his skin tingle. And the dark—he'd forgotten how dark it was on the farm after living for three years with constant electric lights everywhere. The yellow glow from the windows faded as they walked toward the barn. Daad switched on the flashlight he carried, sending a circle of light ahead of them.

Ben tilted his head back. The stars were so bright it seemed he could reach out and touch them. "How bright the stars are here," he said, his breath misting in front of his face.

Daad grunted. "No other lights to dim God's handiwork."

Daad had never lost an opportunity to point out God's presence in their lives. He'd always said that it was a blessing to be a farmer, because it was as close as one could get to Heaven.

But right now, Daad wasn't doing much talking. If they were going to communicate, it was probably up to him.

"You extended the chicken coop, I see."

Daad flickered his flashlight in that direction. "The roof was getting bad, so we decided to replace the whole thing. Just took a day with everyone helping."

Everyone but him, he supposed Daad meant. He couldn't deny that. "I can't believe how Josh has grown. He's a man already."

A grunt of agreement was Daad's only answer. This was going to be an uphill battle. He hurried to shove back the heavy door before Daad reached it.

Their entrance was greeted by soft whickers from the stalls. Daad lit the propane lantern, and the interior of the barn emerged from the gloom.

A wave of emotion hit Ben, startling him by its

strength. Why would he be so moved by the barn? Maybe it was the assurance of Daad's routine. Nothing really needed to be done with the stock at this hour, but still, Daad never went to bed without a last check, just as Mamm had to check each of her *kinder*. Ben had been proud the first time Daad considered him old enough to come along on the evening round.

He stepped to the nearest stall, reaching up to run a hand along the neck of the buggy horse that nosed him curiously. "You're a handsome fellow." He stroked strong shoulders. "The gelding's a good-looking animal. He's new, ain't so?"

"Went all the way down to Lancaster County for the livestock auction last spring to get him."

Daad sounded as proud as an Amish person was likely to, pride being a sin. Funny, how the Englisch world seemed to consider it right and proper.

"Looks like you got a *gut* deal."

He moved to the next stall, to be greeted with a nuzzle that nearly knocked his hat off. Dolly, the black-and-white pony they'd all learned to drive with. Her muzzle was a little gray now, but she looked fine and healthy.

He patted her, letting the memories flood back… driving the pony cart up the road to the neighbor's farm, the day he'd thrown himself on Dolly's back and urged her to gallop, the feel of the ground coming at him when she'd stopped suddenly, objecting to being ridden.

"Suppose I should have sold Dolly to someone with young *kinder*." Daad stood next to him, his gaze on the pony. "But she's *gut* with Daniel's young one when he comes over."

Besides the fact that Daad wouldn't have wanted to part with her. Ben understood that—he wouldn't, either.

"There's something I need to say to you, Benjamin." Daad's voice was weighted with meaning. "Your *mamm* and me…well, we'd always thought that the farm would go to you when we were ready to take it a bit easier. I guess you knew that."

He had, yes. It had been an accepted thing. Amish farms typically went to one of the younger sons, because they came of age when fathers were ready to take it a bit easier. And Ben had been the one who'd loved the farm more than Josh, whose mind was taken up by all things mechanical.

Maybe that had been in his mind that last night, when he'd seen himself settling down, marrying Anna, taking over the farm when it was time, building the next generation. It had closed in on him, reminding him of all the things he hadn't seen, hadn't done.

"Still, when you stayed away so long, we had to face the fact that you might not be back. So we decided the farm would go to Joshua. He's young yet, not settled, but I'm good for a few more years." Daad flickered a glance at him, then focused on Dolly. "Only fair to tell you. I don't think it right to change our minds again. This is still your home, but it'll go to Joshua, not you."

It shouldn't have hit him like a hammer. He should have expected it. After all, it was only right. He'd made his choice when he left.

He forced himself to nod, to smile. "Joshua will do a fine job, I know."

It was only now, when it was out of his reach, that Ben realized how much this place meant to him.

Chapter Three

Anna had no need to cluck to Buck when they came in sight of the Schmidt farm on the way back from home visits a few days later. Buck knew that his own barn would soon be appearing and knew, too, that there'd be a treat for him once he was unhitched.

"Easy, boy." Anna said it with indulgence in her voice. Given the leaden skies and cold temperatures, she'd be glad to get into the warm farmhouse kitchen, rich with the scents of whatever Elizabeth had decided to treat her menfolk with today.

The fencepost that marked the beginning of the Miller fields came in to view, with someone in the usual black coat and black felt hat bending over the post. He looked up and waved, and she saw that it was Ben. She pulled the mare to a halt at his upraised hand.

Ben smiled up at her, lines crinkling around his blue eyes. "A ride home, please?" he asked.

"For sure." She gestured toward the seat next to her.

If he could act as if things were normal between them, so could she.

He climbed up, settling on the seat, and Buck flicked an ear back in recognition of the extra weight.

"*Komm*, Buck, you remember me, ain't so?"

Anna had to smile at his teasing. "He's not used to having another person along on home visit days." Anna snapped the lines, and Buck moved on.

"You've been doing most of them, seems like." Ben shot a glance at her face. "Mamm's all right, isn't she?"

"Ach, ya, she's fine. I think she feels having me take over more of the home visits might push folks into accepting me."

Elizabeth hadn't actually said so, but Anna could read her pretty well. After all, it had always been the understanding between them that Anna would take over more of the practice as Elizabeth wanted to slow down.

"How's that working out?" Ben had a trick of lifting one eyebrow when he asked a question that always seemed to cause a little flutter in her heart.

Anna forced herself to concentrate. "Pretty well, I think. Etta Beachy even let me check out her daughter-in-law today. Reluctantly."

He chuckled. "Sounds like Etta hasn't changed much. Always has to have everything her way, ain't so?"

Anna shrugged. "She wants the best for her first grandbaby." And she didn't think Anna was the best. She didn't say that aloud, of course. And she certain sure didn't confide the thing that was weighing on her.

Elizabeth seemed sure Dora's baby wouldn't arrive until the New Year, and she'd had plenty more experience than Anna had. But based on her examination today, Anna would have guessed a good week or two earlier.

She'd reminded Dora that babies could easily arrive two weeks early or two weeks late, just to have Etta pooh-pooh the notion that her grandson would show up any earlier than the date she'd determined, January 6, Old Christmas, which was her husband's birthday.

Anna hadn't felt up to taking on an argument about the baby's sex, either. She sent Dora a meaningful glance, relieved to see a smile and a shrug in return. Maybe Dora wasn't as cowed by her formidable mother-in-law as she'd thought.

Ben put his hands over hers on the lines, startling her, and she realized they'd nearly run right into the barn, buggy and all.

"Ach, sorry. I was woolgathering." She looped the lines and scrambled down before Ben could offer to help her.

"Problems?" he said lightly, coming around to start the unharnessing.

"No, nothing at all." She kept her head down, focusing on the job at hand.

"I see." He patted the mare's neck. "If you decide to talk to somebody, I know how to keep a secret. And I owe you."

For an instant she was struck dumb. Was he talking about her not saying anything about his phone call? Or was that by way of being an apology to saying he loved her and then vanishing?

If she didn't know, it was surely best to say nothing.

She managed to glance at him with a smile. "Only a midwife's menfolk would find it possible to talk about the birth of a *boppli* in mixed company."

Ben grinned. "The rest of them pretend they don't even notice a babe is coming until it is safe in its cradle."

As Anna reached up to pull off the headstall, Ben grabbed it first. "You go in and warm up," he said. "I've got this."

"But you don't know about Buck's treat when he is unharnessed," she said lightly. "You might make a mistake and try to give him a carrot."

"He's a fussy one, is he?" Ben pulled the harness free. "What is it? A sugar cube?"

"That's right." Anna held it on her palm, feeling Buck's soft lips brushing her skin as he took the sugar.

"Spoiled thing," Ben teased.

"A midwife's buggy horse has to be ready for a lot of unexpected trips," she said. "He works for his sugar."

Anna led the gelding toward the paddock while Ben carried the harness to its rack. It was easy, it seemed, to get back to the kind of teasing conversation she'd once had with Ben. Too easy? She couldn't risk falling for him all over again.

Opening the gate, she released the horse. Buck trotted a few steps and then stopped, lifting his head and sniffing the air.

Snow! Anna saw the first few flakes nearly as soon as the horse did. She tilted her head back, scanning the sky for more.

"What are you doing?" Ben had reached the gate without her noticing.

"Snow," she said, unable to keep the glee from her voice.

Ben chuckled. "I'd near forgot that you're like a kid when it snows." A sudden breeze sent a cluster of snowflakes dancing across the paddock. Buck whinnied, pranced in place for a moment and then trotted around in a circle, head tossing.

Ben laughed. "Or maybe like the horse. Sure you don't want to run around in a circle, too?"

"Nothing wrong with getting excited about the first snow." She could hear the defensiveness in her voice.

Ben clasped her by the wrists, and she looked up at his face. "Nothing at all wrong," he said gently. "I'm glad of it, Anna. Makes me feel like I could shed a few burdens and trot around, too."

Still holding her wrists, he swung her around, his face lit with laughter. "We'll both celebrate, ain't so?"

Laughing, Anna swung around with him, face tilted back to feel the flakes on her skin, until she was breathless.

"Stop, stop." She grabbed his forearms, feeling solid muscle under the layers of fabric. "What if someone saw us?"

"They'd think we were a bit *ferhoodled*." He stopped, so suddenly she might have fallen if not for his strong hands holding hers.

For an instant they stood staring at each other, and she felt her heart turn over. Then he was stepping away. "We'd best get inside and get warmed up. Josh will be wanting to get the sleigh out if this keeps up."

He sounded perfectly normal, as if he'd felt nothing at all in that moment when her heart had twisted.

Anna took a deep breath of cold air, knowing her cheeks were burning. So. She'd told herself she could get back to the way they'd been before the night she'd known she loved him. She'd been wrong. Their relationship was a lot more complicated than that.

"I'm telling you, Ben, this is going to be a great winter for snow. Grossdaadi says the woolly bear caterpillars predicted a real snowy winter. We have to get the sleigh ready."

Grinning, Ben followed his younger brother up the ladder to the upper loft in the barn. In some ways Josh, despite his size, was still the little kid brother he'd always been.

"Okay, okay, I said I'd help you get the sleigh ready and I will. Just don't blame me if it sits high and dry for half the winter."

"It won't," Josh said confidently, scrambling the rest of the way into the loft and reaching back a gloved hand to tug Ben up beside him.

"There she is," Josh said proudly. "Let's get it uncovered and down to the barn floor."

"Easier said than done." Ben gave a mock grumble, but truth to tell, he'd have done something a lot harder to have this time to get reacquainted with his little brother.

Together they rigged up the sleigh to the hook used to move bales and lowered it to the floor. Josh was so eager to get at it that he would have tumbled down the ladder if not for Ben's steadying hand.

"Take it easy. The sleigh's not going anywhere."

"I know." Josh grinned. "Boy, it's *gut* to have you home again." He sobered, as if wondering whether that was the right thing to say.

Ben gripped his shoulder for a moment. "Me, too." Regret swept over him. He'd let Josh down when he'd left, not even thinking of him. Dan and Joseph were enough older that Josh would never have confided in them. There seemed no end to the lives affected by his leaving.

Josh chattered as they worked on the sleigh, wiping away the dust that had accumulated over the summer and removing every speck of rust from the runners. "And besides, Anna loves to take the sleigh out. She'll be surprised when she sees it's ready. Anna does so much for everyone, I want to do something nice for her. She really is like a big sister to me." He sent a side-long glance at Ben, as if to see how he was taking that.

Ben figured the safest thing he could do was nod. Obviously everyone in the family would have been happy if he and Anna had married. He couldn't marry to make other people happy, but given how strong an attraction she still had for him, maybe…

No maybes, he told himself. Whatever he did or didn't do here, he couldn't hurt Anna again.

"Anna says…" Josh paused, polishing vigorously at an already shining runner.

When he didn't go on, Ben elbowed him. "Go ahead. What does Anna say?"

Josh rubbed even harder. "She says I should just tell you what I feel."

What now? "Go ahead." He braced himself.

"I guess Daad told you about his plans for the farm?"

"Ya, and it's fine." He hastened to assure him, hoping he sounded convincing. "You deserve it. I'm happy for you."

"But that's just it." The words burst out of Josh. "I'm not happy. I don't want it." He clamped his lips shut and glanced around as if afraid someone had heard.

Ben felt a frown knotting his forehead. "But how can you not want a farm like this?"

"You say that because it's your dream," Josh said. "Just like it's Daad's. Nobody understands that I might want something different."

Josh's voice had risen, and Ben put his hand on the boy's arm.

"Hey, it's okay. Just tell me what you want."

"What I always wanted. You know I always liked working with machines better than anything. I'm the one who fixed the generator when it stopped, remember? And I rebuilt that baler when everyone else gave up on it, too."

He couldn't help but be moved by the passion in Josh's voice. "If you feel that way about it, won't Daad understand?"

"I tried. He just doesn't see. He thinks it's fair that I have the farm, and he won't change his mind." Josh turned his face away, obviously not wanting anyone to see his emotion.

Here was something else to be laid to his account, it seemed. But what could he do? A look at his brother forced a decision. He had to make this right for Josh, somehow.

He grasped his brother by the shoulders and shook him gently. "Listen, we'll work it out somehow. Let me think on it, okay? There must be a way."

"*Denke*, Ben." Josh's expression lightened. "Anna said I should talk to you, and she was right. She always seems to understand."

In other words, Anna had been trying to fill the gap he'd left in his little brother's life. He wanted to resent it, but he couldn't. Anna had paid him a compliment, in a way. She'd trusted he'd find a way to make this right for Josh. He just hoped her faith wasn't mistaken.

Chapter Four

Anna sliced through the dough on the cutting board, turning out the homemade noodle squares that Elizabeth would drop into her chicken potpie. They'd been able to come home early today, with few people venturing out into the snow.

Trying to keep her mind on Elizabeth's voice wasn't easy when her thoughts were completely absorbed by those moments with Ben out by the paddock the previous day. His laughing face as he'd spun her around had even intruded into her dreams. There, she'd been spinning faster and faster until she flew against him and his arms closed around her.

She had to stop this, now. Benjamin had been so frightened at the thought of marrying her that he'd left his whole world behind. It was hardly likely his feelings had changed now.

"I said, it's a *gut* thing no one is due today or tomorrow," Elizabeth said…or rather, repeated, since it was apparent that Anna hadn't heard her before.

Focus, Anna ordered herself. "That's certain sure. We don't need any women in labor bouncing around trying to get here through the snow."

Once the snow had decided to start, it hadn't let up, and there was four inches at least on the ground. They'd have a quiet time of it until the roads were clear, and it always took some time for the township plows to arrive.

Anna rubbed her forehead with the back of her hand, trying not to touch anything with her floury fingers. Unless she wanted to go around in a constant state of confusion, she'd have to find a way to show Ben that she didn't harbor any lingering feelings for him. Then they could be comfortable together, couldn't they?

"*Komm*, Anna, tell me what has your forehead so tight? That's the third time you've rubbed it in the past half hour." Elizabeth stirred down the chicken broth that had come to a boil. "I know when you're worried."

But she'd never guess the cause of Anna's worry, and Anna didn't dare tell her. "Ach, it's nothing. I was just thinking about Dora Beachy. I'm concerned that *boppli* might be arriving sooner than anyone expects."

"Ya?" Elizabeth turned to her instantly. "Did you say anything to her?"

"I didn't like to, since she's really your patient. I did remind them that babies can arrive two weeks early or two weeks late and still be normal."

Elizabeth nodded approval. "That was the smart thing to say. Of course, a first baby is more likely to be late than early."

"I know." But still, she was troubled. What if they didn't send for help in time?

"Tell you what," Elizabeth said, seeming to read her thoughts. "I'll stop over next week and check on Dora. That will make everyone feel better, ain't so?"

Anna let out a breath of relief. "I'd be so glad. Maybe I'm…"

Before she could finish the thought, they were interrupted by the soft sound of hooves on snow and the jingle of harness bells. Together they rushed to the back porch to find Josh and Benjamin grinning at them from the high seat of the sleigh. Ben held the lines, while Josh jiggled a strap of tiny bells.

"So that's what you two boys have been up to all afternoon." Elizabeth smiled fondly at her sons. "I should have known."

"Get your coats on, you two. We're going to take you for a ride." Josh jumped down to hustle them along. "Hurry up. You first, Mamm."

"Ach, I'm too old for such foolishness," Elizabeth protested, but halfheartedly.

"Never," Anna exclaimed, rushing to retrieve their coats and mittens.

Since the sleigh was a two-seater, Josh took his mother up beside him to the accompaniment of a string of warnings from his *daad*, who came out of the barn to join the fun. They went sliding off down the snow-covered lane, the snow muffling the sound of the horse's hooves.

"Don't worry, Daad." Ben stamped snow from his feet. "He'll be careful with Mamm."

"When you boys start playing around with the sleigh,

you forget all about being careful," Asa said, but he was smiling as he watched. "Mind you don't go speeding when you take Anna."

It hadn't occurred to Anna that logically Ben would take her for a ride since Josh had done the first trip. She was still trying to find a way to get out of it when the sleigh came sweeping back, Elizabeth laughing like a girl. Before Anna knew what was happening, she'd been bundled up onto the seat beside Ben.

He shot her a mischievous grin. "We'll show them how it's done, ain't so?"

"You heard your *daad*," she began, then gave it up as Ben guided the sleigh in a broad circle and she had to grasp the side rail to keep from sliding right off the seat.

Ben sent the gelding off toward the woods at a brisk pace, and she held tightly.

"We're not racing, are we?" She tried to sound stern, but the question came out on a giggle. She couldn't help it—it was so exhilarating to fly noiselessly over the snow, the breeze sending flakes to dust her coat and melt against her skin.

"Fun, ain't so?" Ben smiled at her again, and her heart seemed to flip in her chest.

"You might say you did this for Joshua's sake, but we all know better. You wanted to play in the snow as much as he did."

"You're just the same. Remember how excited you got yesterday at the first flakes?" His voice was low and teasing, and Anna had to struggle not to meet his eyes.

"I confess. We're all kids about something, ain't so?"

Ben nodded, but for some reason the words seemed

to set up a more serious line of thought for him. They'd nearly reached the woods, where the farm lane ended, and he drew the buggy to a stop.

With the snow muffling every sound, Anna felt as if they were alone in the world. She had to say something.

"The…the hemlocks are beautiful in the snow. Look how it's bending the branches down. It's as if they're…"

"Anna." His voice was low, but it halted her foolish chatter in an instant. "There's something I must say to you. I've owed you an apology for three years, and I haven't been able to find the words to tell you how sorry I am."

"Don't, Ben. Don't." She put out her hand to stop him and then realized it was much safer not to touch him. But she saw, quite suddenly, what she must say to ease the tension between them.

"It worked out for the best, ain't so? I don't mean you going away, but the fact that we didn't get together." Anna took a breath of cold air and forced herself to go on. "Moonlight and kisses don't make a solid basis for marriage. We're such completely different people now."

Her throat was getting so tight that she didn't think she could say anything more, but maybe that was enough. She risked a glance at Ben's face, but his somber expression didn't tell her anything.

Finally he nodded. "If you feel you can forgive me, that's all that counts. I hope we can be friends again."

Anna forced herself to smile. "Friends." That was all she could manage, but it seemed to be enough.

Ben clucked to the horse and they turned back toward the farmhouse.

* * *

Ben did his best not to fidget as the three-hour Sunday morning service drew near the end. He'd been trying to efface himself, in the hope he could fade into the mass of black-coated men. What a wimp he'd turned into while he was away—after all, he'd grown up sitting on the backless benches for worship, and he didn't even remember thinking it was that hard.

Hard was definitely the word for this bench. He shifted his weight slightly and earned a frown from his eldest brother, Daniel. Dan had always felt responsible for the younger ones, and that didn't seem to have changed. His greeting had been restrained, and he'd glanced at Daad as if taking his cue from him. Joseph, so close in age to Daniel that they might as well have been twins, had followed his lead, but as they'd lined up to enter the basement when worship was being held, Joe had given him a quick smile and a wink that warmed his heart.

You didn't expect this to be easy, he reminded himself. It seemed he was saying that a lot lately.

The final prayer, the final hymn, and the long service was over. Bishop John King, passing close as he moved through the congregation, inclined his head gravely. Ben nodded back, guessing what the bishop was thinking—that if Ben intended to stay, he'd have to make his confession before the church. It was an intimidating thought, but the forgiveness granted to the sinner afterward was sincere and complete. The wrong was wiped out as if it had never been.

Daad put a hand on his shoulder. "Not until you're

ready," he said softly. "Meantime, help the boys set up the tables for lunch, *ja*?"

Ben's throat tightened. Daad, for all his strictness with his boys, had always seemed to understand. If he ever had a family, would he have that gift? *If.*

"Here, Ben, give us a hand." Joe and Dan were making short work of converting the benches to the tables that would seat them for the after-church meal. "Or have you forgot how?"

Ben grinned at the familiar joshing and grabbed the end of the table Josh was struggling with. "Josh and I will get more done than you two. Come on, Josh." Together they raised the wooden planks easily, fitting them into the brackets that turned them into tables. Typical Amish ingenuity, he thought. The benches and tables had to be hauled from one home to the next for services, so why not make the best use of them?

Already some of the women were carrying bowls and platters down the stairs from the Fisher family's kitchen. Each family took a turn to host worship, but it only made sense to do winter worship at a home that had a warm, dry basement instead of a barn.

They were finishing the last table when Ben spotted Anna coming down, her arms around a huge coffee urn. Anna had made it easy for him to forgive himself for the hurt he'd offered her. At least he didn't have to worry about that. So why didn't her rational acceptance make him feel more content?

"Let me take that." He discovered he'd moved to help Anna before he'd consciously decided on it. He grabbed the urn. "It's heavy."

For an instant she resisted, but then she let go and smiled. "Over here on the end of the table," she said, gesturing to the long table that was already becoming covered with the fixings of the after-church lunch.

He set it down in the spot she indicated. "I see…" Ben lost his train of thought when he heard his mother's name, coming from a small knot of women a few yards away.

"…saying that it's not fair for Elizabeth Miller to just stop doing her home visits. She's our midwife, and she shouldn't be pushing us off on someone second-best, like Anna Zook."

Ben recognized Etta Beachy's strident voice even though her back was to them. Obviously some things didn't change. Etta was known as the biggest *blabbermaul* in the church district.

He didn't realize he'd taken a step toward the woman until he felt Anna's hand on his arm. She shook her head.

"Don't say anything," she murmured. "Your *mamm* wouldn't like it, and I don't need defending." Her smile flickered. "Your *mamm* would say that the irritating people in the church are sent to teach the rest of us patience."

Ben gave a reluctant nod. Anna was right, and that sounded exactly like his mother. But still, he didn't like to hear the woman talking that way about Mamm. And what made her so sure that Anna was second-best?

It seemed he'd lost some of his patience while he was living Englisch. He put his hand over hers and squeezed it lightly. "If so, Etta fills the role to perfection, ain't so?"

Anna tried to suppress a giggle and didn't quite succeed. Her eyes danced even as she shook her head at him.

How could he have ever thought her plain? When her face lit with laughter, she had an elusive beauty that intrigued him.

Whoa, don't go there. He eased his hand away from hers. "*Denke.* For keeping me out of trouble."

She glanced away, and a slight flush rose in her cheeks.

"And imagine that Ben Miller, sitting in worship like he belonged there." Etta apparently wasn't finished with his family yet. "He ought to be in the penitent seat. Why hasn't he confessed?"

Interestingly, two of the women had drifted away, maybe not wanting to be associated with Etta's views. The one who was left tried in vain to shush her with an agonized glance in their direction.

To Ben's surprise, he felt Anna stiffen at his side. Was she really angrier at the slight to him than at the reflection on herself? Of course, knowing Anna, he suspected she wouldn't admit to being angry at all. But she couldn't deny the way her eyes snapped or the flush on her cheekbones.

Oddly enough, that amused him. "Relax," he whispered. "I'll show you how to deal with the Ettas of the world."

Not looking back, he strode over to Etta and her embarrassed companion, hearing a small gasp from behind him.

"Etta Beachy. It's nice to see you after all this time."

He produced a smile. "And this must be Sally Fisher, ain't so?"

Sally nodded, her color high. "*Gut* to see you home again, Benjamin. *Wilkom* back."

Etta, obviously not sure what he might have overheard, pressed her lips together into a thin line. For a moment he thought she wouldn't say anything, but then she gave a short nod. "Your *mamm* must be pleased to see you after all this time."

"Three years," he said, determined not to let her ruffle him. "I see you haven't changed a bit." *Still as big a blabbermaul as ever*, he thought.

Something that might have been a chuckle escaped Sally. He nodded to each of them before heading for the table where Daad and his brothers were waiting. But on the way he couldn't resist a glance back at Anna.

She shook her head at him, but her eyes twinkled. Maybe he'd taken the sting out of Etta's comments for her.

Another thought struck him as he took his place at the table and he thought again of her reaction to the criticism of him. Perhaps Anna wasn't quite as indifferent to him as she wanted him to believe.

Chapter Five

The snow was gone from the roads by the time Elizabeth and Anna set out for the Beachy home on Monday afternoon. A brisk wind ripped snow from the trees and sent it swirling in front of the buggy horse who plodded patiently on. Anna was glad of the blanket over their knees, and she tucked it in more snugly.

"Are you sure you want me to be with you on this visit?" she asked, hoping she wasn't repeating herself. "I mean, Etta and Dora might feel freer to talk if I'm not there."

"I've never noticed anything keeping Etta from talking," Elizabeth said. She took her gaze from the road long enough to study Anna's face. "Are you worried that I won't agree with you?"

"Not worried, exactly." But Etta's comment referring to her as second-best seemed lodged in her mind, despite Ben's efforts. "I'll be glad to have your opinion. Maybe I'm wrong, and if so..."

Elizabeth startled her by reaching over to grasp

her hand. "None of that, now. Whether we are right or wrong in a particular situation, we must always take the course that's safest for the *mammi* and the *boppli*."

"Even if it makes me look foolish?"

"Even so." Elizabeth smiled. "And not just you. I mind one time when I was so sure I'd heard a second heartbeat. I told the parents, and they rushed around borrowing an extra cradle and getting more blankets and diapers."

"And?" She suspected how this story was going to play out by the way Elizabeth's eyes twinkled.

"Nobody was more surprised than me when I delivered one big, healthy boy. I never have figured out what it was I heard that day." She chuckled. "I was a long time living that down, believe me."

Anna squeezed her hand before letting go. "You're just trying to make me feel better."

"Is it working?" Elizabeth asked innocently.

They were both still laughing when they drove up the lane to the farmhouse.

Etta must have been watching for them. One of the boys ran out to take the horse and offer a hand to help Elizabeth down. Anna jumped down herself, her sturdy shoes landing on the hard-packed snow of the lane. She picked up the medical bag and followed Elizabeth to the back door.

"*Komm* in, *komm* in." Etta was there to greet them. She gave Anna a sidelong glance and addressed Elizabeth. "We didn't know you were both coming."

Elizabeth's smile didn't falter. "I think it best if both of us see every patient a few times. We're partners, after all. If one of us should be busy with another *mammi* when someone goes into labor, we should both be familiar with the case, ain't so?"

Etta didn't look convinced, but she didn't argue, to Anna's relief. Was she feeling a bit guilty after being caught gossiping? Or wondering if Elizabeth had heard about her criticism of Ben? It was certain sure Elizabeth hadn't heard it from either her or Ben, but very often she seemed to know what was happening without being told.

The two of them shed their outer garments, hanging coats and bonnets on the pegs near the back door. Rubbing her palms together, Elizabeth moved to the gas heater in the corner.

"Dora won't want us touching her with cold hands, ain't so?" She smiled at Dora, sitting near the heater in a padded rocker. "How are you feeling?"

"Fine, fine." Dora glanced at her mother-in-law. "Mamm Etta is taking *gut* care of me."

Etta beamed. "Ach, we're all wonderful happy about the baby coming."

There was a little more chitchat, restrained on Etta's part and careful on Anna's, but Elizabeth chattered normally, drawing Dora out on the progress of her pregnancy. It was fascinating to see Dora relax and gain assurance under the influence of her warmth.

That was a place where she needed to improve, Anna decided. Conquering her natural shyness was a day-by-day battle, but she had to keep at it if she was going to be the midwife Elizabeth was.

They all adjourned to the bedroom, where Elizabeth gave Dora a swift, deft exam. Anna, holding the girl's hand, saw the apprehension in her eyes. "It's all right," she said, patting her shoulder. "Everything is fine."

Catching the words, Elizabeth looked up and smiled. "That's certain sure. It won't be long until you're holding this little *boppli* in your arms."

"How soon?" Etta chimed in.

Elizabeth chuckled. "*Komm*, Etta, you know better than to ask me to pinpoint the birth date. All yours were a bit late, as I recall."

"For sure. I thought James was never going to get here." Etta shot a glance at Anna, as if to say, *you see?*

"'Course Dora isn't going to take after you. Could be anytime from two weeks early to two weeks late and still be normal." She patted Dora's belly. "Just let us know if you start having any contractions or even feeling not quite right. That's what we're here for, and one of us will always come."

Dora nodded, her small face relaxing, and she smoothed her hand over her belly protectively. "James and I pray for a healthy baby, whenever it arrives."

"*Gut*. That's the best way to think." Elizabeth nodded to Anna. "We'd best be on our way. It's turning colder, I think."

Naturally Etta didn't want to let them go without giving them coffee and cake, and they finally compromised by taking a thermos of coffee with them.

"It'll be most *wilkom* on the way home," Elizabeth said, and pushed Anna gently out the door.

The wind caught them as they left the shelter of the porch, and they scurried to the buggy that James had ready and waiting for them. In another moment they were on the road home.

"Brr." Elizabeth tucked the blanket more firmly over

them. "It's turning colder. The snow will stay to make it a white Christmas, I think."

"That sounds lovely to me." Anna glanced at her. "But tell me the truth. You don't agree with me about Dora's baby coming earlier, do you?"

"You heard what I told Dora. Besides, babies have a mind of their own when it comes to that. Still, I can see why you think it." Elizabeth gave a little nod. "Dora is carrying low and in front, just like her *mamm* did. Makes her look as if the little one is about to pop out. But hers usually arrived right about their due date."

Anna nodded, a little relieved though still wondering. "It's a shame Dora's family moved out to Ohio when they did. She'd like having her *mamm* here."

"I'm sure that's so. Although Etta was a bit less opinionated today than she usually is. I almost asked her if she were sick."

Anna was surprised into a laugh. "Ach, I shouldn't laugh at her, but…" She stopped, thinking it might be best not to bring up the subject of Ben's encounter with Etta.

"Something happened after worship Sunday, ain't so?"

"How…" Anna stared at her.

"How do I know?" Elizabeth finished for her. "Because I have eyes in my head." She sighed, staring straight ahead toward the horse's ears. "I was keeping watch on Benjamin, of course. Couldn't help it—I wanted so much for him to feel as if he fits in again."

Anna's mind stumbled over how to respond. "I don't think he would be upset by anything Etta might say. He knows what she's like."

"Ach, sometimes I have thoughts that aren't very Christian about that woman." Elizabeth clutched the lines so tightly that the mare turned her head to look back, as if asking why.

"I know. But Ben took it in stride. He even had me laughing about it."

"I'm wonderful glad you were with him. You always seemed to understand Ben so well." Elizabeth reached out to clasp her hand. "Please, just keep being a friend to him. Encourage him. He needs that right now. Will you?"

Be a friend. Encourage him. And how was she to protect her heart while she was doing that?

But she didn't really have a choice. She squeezed Elizabeth's hand. "Of course I will."

"Slide in there." Ben's brother Daniel gave him a nudge that sent him along the bench at the back of the schoolroom a few nights later. Dan and his wife, holding their two young kids, came in after him, pushing him farther as the rest of the family piled in behind them.

It was the night of the Amish school Christmas program, and even though the family no longer had *kinder* in the school, they wouldn't think of missing it. In fact, there was about as good a turnout for the program as there was for Sunday worship.

Dan pressed him a bit more as he made room, and Ben found himself crunched up against Anna. Not that he minded, but he wasn't sure how Anna would take it. However, she just smiled and slid her coat under the bench to make a bit more space.

"Close quarters," he murmured. "Looks like the whole church is here."

"For sure. No one would want to miss seeing the

scholars say their Christmas pieces." She reached out as Dan's two-year-old, Reuben, wiggled his way over adult knees to reach her. "Want to sit on my lap?"

He nodded, one finger in his mouth, and gave Ben a sidelong look as if not sure what to make of this new *onkel* of his. When Anna lifted him, he snuggled against her, still staring at Ben.

Anna ruffled the boy's corn silk hair and whispered to him. "That's Onkel Ben, remember? Can you give him a smile?"

Reuben pulled the finger out of his mouth just long enough to produce a smile, dimples appearing in his rosy cheeks. Then, apparently stricken by shyness, he buried his face in the front of Anna's dress.

Ben wasn't sure whether to find it funny or not. "Guess he's not ready to accept me just yet."

"He's a little shy, like most two-year-olds," Anna said. "Give him time." She stroked Reuben's head lightly. "Besides, it's already past his bedtime."

"I won't push."

That had to be his motto for everything about his return. Relationships might be easy to break but they could be hard to rebuild. Maybe it would be easier with Reuben and his baby sister, since they weren't old enough to have been disappointed by him.

"I thought I heard your voice." The guy ahead of him turned around, a grin splitting his face. "Ben. *Wilkom* back!" Gus Schmidt, once one of his closest friends, pounded him on the shoulder. "Sure is *gut* to see you."

"I'm wonderful glad to be here. You've changed." Ben nodded toward the bristly beard that adorned Gus's chin.

"I'm an old married man by now. Nancy finally put me out of my misery."

Nancy Fisher and Gus had been sweethearts already when Ben left, so he wasn't surprised. But it did startle him to see the *boppli* Gus held on his knee. The little girl babbled, reaching past him toward Reuben.

"This here's Mary Grace." He bounced the tot on his knee and she grinned, showing her few teeth.

Ben shook his head. "Imagine you, responsible enough to be a *daadi*. I never thought I'd see the day."

"Beat you to it, anyway." Gus looked as if he couldn't stop smiling.

The familiar give and take between buddies was a balm to his heart. Here was one person, at least, who hadn't changed in his regard.

"If Nancy knew half the things you got up to, she'd never trust you with a *boppli*. Where is Nancy, anyway?"

"She's been helping out with the props for the program. She'd want to talk to you later, but mind you don't say anything about the mischief you led me into. I had enough sense not to…"

Gus let that trail off, and the tips of his ears reddened. "I mean…"

"It's okay." Ben punched his arm lightly. If he was going to stay, he'd have to get used to folks stumbling over what to say about his jumping the fence. "I always did have to learn everything the hard way, ain't so?"

The teacher walked to the front of the audience just then, and everyone got quiet, sparing Gus the embarrassment of answering. "We'll get together later, ain't so?" he murmured, and turned to face front.

Ben settled back onto the bench and realized that

Anna was watching his face, maybe measuring how much he was affected by that conversation. He gave her a reassuring smile and watched her flush a little in return.

Teacher Lydia proved to be Nancy's younger sister. She had more poise than he'd have expected as she welcomed everyone and introduced the program. As usual, the evening began with the youngest scholars, probably because they were too excited to wait.

He might have expected to be bored by the program, given some of the entertainment he'd seen in the outside world. In fact, he was completely rapt. The scholars' innocent faces, intent expressions and sometimes wobbly voices were enchanting. He glanced at Anna. She was watching just as closely, a reminiscent smile curving her lips.

Of course it would be familiar to her. Even though she hadn't grown up in Lost Creek, her school would have had a program that was probably very like this one. No doubt she'd stood up in front of the audience, quaking a bit, to say her lines.

As if Anna felt his gaze, she met his eyes.

"Do you miss it?" he whispered under cover of the song the younger *kinder* were singing. "Being with your own folks at Christmastime?"

She shook her head. "I was there visiting at Thanksgiving. But Lost Creek is home now. And I get out of the *rumspringa* gang Christmas parties."

That comment startled him. Why wouldn't she want to get together with the girls she'd gone through *rumspringa* with? Those were usually the people who became your friends for life.

Then he really looked at her, seeing what he hadn't

before. She cradled the sleeping Reuben against her heart, and when she looked down at him, her face was suffused with tenderness. Of course. All those girls would have families by now, except for Anna. And she wanted a family—that shone so clearly in her face.

Ben's breath seemed to catch in his throat. She was so loving and so very lovely as she watched his nephew. He saw her as he'd seen her that night so long ago, when he'd realized without warning that he loved her.

And then he'd panicked at the thought of what that meant—giving up the travels he dreamed of, settling down to the same life as his father and his brothers, with all hope of adventure gone. He'd panicked. And he'd run.

Anna glanced up and caught him looking at her. Her eyes widened, and a tiny pulse beat at her temple. He couldn't look away. Their gazes were entangled. He couldn't see anything but her face, hear anything but the breath she took. It was as if they were alone in the room.

Maybe it was *gut* that they weren't alone, or he'd never be able to stop himself from drawing her into his arms, kissing her sweet lips, holding her tight—

The cell phone he'd put in his jacket began to vibrate. He could switch it off. Ignore it. That's what he'd been trying to do since he came home, but it wasn't working.

He'd left unfinished business behind in the outside world, and it wasn't going to leave him alone. The truth hit him like a blow. He'd never be able to commit fully to the church, to his family or to Anna until he'd made things right with Mickey.

Chapter Six

Breakfast at the Miller house was never a quiet affair, since Josh always had something to talk about. Today his *mamm* was busy teasing him about his efforts to help Teacher Lydia at the program the previous night. Given the way the tips of his ears had turned red, there had been more to his helpfulness than just pitching in.

Anna sent a cautious glance at Ben. Although he was smiling at his brother's plight, he seemed a bit preoccupied. Was he thinking of those moments at the Christmas program when it seemed their hearts had touched? Or was that just her imagination? And how many times did she have to remind herself that Ben had broken her heart once already? It would be foolish to give him an opportunity to do it again.

"How many appointments are scheduled for the birthing center today, Anna?" Elizabeth settled at the foot of the table, nursing a second cup of coffee and leafing through her box of handwritten recipes.

Anna had to scramble to get her thoughts back to business. "I have two, and I think you might have three."

"Is that what you'd call a baby boom, Mamm?" Ben looked up from his plate of fried scrapple.

"No, just the Amish doing what comes naturally," Elizabeth replied, smiling at him.

Anna found herself smiling, as well. Most Amish males didn't mention a baby until it was safely in its cradle for all to see, but the family of a midwife didn't have such scruples.

Elizabeth pulled a card from the box. "There's my *pfeffernuesse* recipe. I wondered where it got to." She set it on the table with a decided air. "You can take all the appointments today, Anna, ain't so?"

Blinking with surprise, Anna nodded. "I guess so. Aren't you feeling well?"

"I'm feeling like playing hooky and baking Christmas cookies today." Her eyes twinkled. "After all, that's why I have a partner."

Anna did a mental run-through of today's appointments. "Some of your mothers might not like seeing me instead of you," she ventured.

"Well, that's too bad, but they'd best start getting used to it. Sooner or later you'll be taking over completely, ain't so? It's time they started seeing you as the midwife. And maybe time you were convinced of it, too."

She thought she had been. Anna tried not to feel hurt and planted a smile on her face. "I'll take care of it. *Denke*, Elizabeth."

By the time the routine had actually started at the birthing center, Anna had convinced herself that Elizabeth was only trying to bolster her confidence. She did need to show a little more conviction in her abilities, she supposed, but it was comforting to know that Elizabeth was there if she ran into difficulties.

It had wondered her sometimes if giving birth herself would make her more qualified to help others. But since that was unlikely to happen, she'd just have to push through with what she knew and had experienced in the past five years of working with Elizabeth.

The day wore on with no unpleasant surprises. She'd just waved goodbye to one of her Englisch clients when she spotted Ben heading toward the birthing center. She waited on the tiny porch, wrapping a shawl around her against the cold, crisp air. As Ben neared, she could hear the snow crunching under his boots.

"What brings you this way?" she asked, half expecting he'd walk on past to the field beyond.

Instead he mounted the steps, brandishing a toolbox in one hand. "Mamm sent me over to mend the drawer in your desk. She says if you pull on it too hard, it flies out into your lap."

"True enough, but if you have something else to do..."

"Not a thing," he said cheerfully, grabbing the door and holding it for her before following her inside. "Besides, if I hang around the scent of Mamm's baking any longer, I'll be sneaking even more cookies than Joshua is."

"That might be hard." She replaced the shawl on the wall hook where it belonged. "That boy has a sweet tooth, that's certain sure."

Ben gestured to the desk. "Okay if I start work, or do you need to get something out?"

"Just let me grab these files." She picked them up.

"I'll work at your mother's desk until the next patient comes."

The next patient, she reminded herself, was Martha Esch, all of whose eight kinder had been delivered by Elizabeth. Somehow she didn't think Martha was going to be eager to change.

"Problem, is she?" Ben seemed to be reading her mind.

She shrugged. "She's one of your *mamm*'s clients. She may not be too happy about seeing me instead." That didn't sound self-pitying, did it? That was the last thing she wanted.

Ben slid the drawer out, emptying the contents on the desk. "Sounds as if Mamm might be right to push the baby bird out of the nest."

Anna's rare temper flared. "I am not a baby bird."

Ben gave her the teasing grin that melted hearts. "I'm the bird that flew the nest too soon. Which is worse?"

Fortunately for Anna, she heard the sound of a buggy pulling up outside. Chin held high, she went to the door to greet Martha Esch.

Martha came in stamping snow from her shoes. "Nippy out today, ain't so, Anna?" She nodded to Ben. "Wonderful *gut* that you're home, Ben. And making yourself useful, I see."

Anna took her coat and hung it from a hook as Martha removed her bonnet and glanced around. "Where is Elizabeth? I have the time right, don't I?"

"Sure you do." Anna took a breath, wishing Ben were not there listening. "She's taking the day off, and she wants me to see her patients. If you'll *komm* to the other room…"

Martha frowned. "Is she sick?"

"No, nothing like that. She deserves a day off now and then, ain't so?"

"I suppose so." She frowned. "Maybe I'll make my appointment for another day, when she's back. After all, she's been the one to catch all my babies. What about tomorrow?" Martha reached for her coat.

Anna very nearly picked up the appointment calendar. She'd tried, hadn't she? Her hand stilled. She was aware of Martha waiting and of Ben, listening despite his pretense of being absorbed in his work.

What did they see when they looked at her? More importantly, what did she see when she looked in the mirror? How could she expect other people to take her seriously if she didn't take herself that way?

She picked up the patient file and turned to Martha with a smile that was as confident as she could manage. "Elizabeth wants me to check you today. I'll make sure that she sees all the notes from the visit. Shall we go in?" She held the door to the exam room.

Martha stared at her for a moment. Then she shrugged, smiling. "Ach, I'm being foolish, ain't so?" And she walked into the exam room.

Trying not to look surprised, Anna somehow couldn't keep herself from glancing at Ben. His eyes crinkled, and he gave her a thumbs-up sign.

Feeling ridiculously triumphant, Anna went to do her job.

Ben stepped carefully from one plank to another in the attic after supper, well aware that he could go through to the bedroom ceiling if he didn't stay on the boards. Josh, with his usual exuberance, was already under the eaves, shifting boxes.

"I thought Mamm said the crèche set was in a small box," Ben said, knowing that he'd have to restack whatever Josh moved.

"Guess so." Josh shifted the battery lantern he was carrying to illuminate another section of attic. Days were too short now to get much light coming through the small windows.

Ben paused, reaching overhead to rest his hand against the rough-hewn timber that made up the rafters. The first of the Miller family to settle here had built the farmhouse from trees he felled when he cleared land for crops. Ben had always figured that made the old farmhouse as much a part of the land as the huge oak tree behind the barn.

"Not here," Josh said, swinging around. "Better try the other side."

"And you'd best be careful where you step," Ben warned. "I'm not taking the blame if you put your big foot through the bedroom ceiling."

"Remember when Dan did that?" Josh grinned. "I was just a kid, but I can still hear Daad yelling."

"And a bit later it was Dan yelling," Ben said. It had been a long time since he'd reminisced with his brother. It felt good.

"Here it is," Josh said, swinging the lantern over a stack of boxes. He picked up the small box and handed it to Ben.

"Sure enough." The box was labeled in Mamm's meticulous hand. "How did it get way back there anyway? I'd think Mamm would have put it away close to the ladder last year."

Josh didn't answer for a moment. "Mamm hasn't decorated for Christmas much the past few years." He wasn't looking at Ben as he made his way toward the ladder.

It took a moment to sink in, and then Ben's heart sank. Yet another thing to chalk up to his account, it seemed. "Sorry." His voice roughened. "Guess I caused even more trouble than I thought. I hope you and I are okay."

"Sure thing." Once again Josh hesitated. "Have you thought about talking to Daad about the farm and what I want to do? I figured maybe we'd have it settled by now."

He'd thought about it plenty. He just didn't have any answers. "I haven't been back long. Maybe it's best to wait."

"I can't wait." The edge in Josh's voice startled him. "Zeb King is going to take on another apprentice at his machine shop in January, and he gave me first chance at it."

Ben studied his brother's face. "Are you sure that's what you want?" Zeb King had one of the largest Amish-owned businesses in Lost Creek, doing all kinds of machine work for Englisch companies.

"Not for good. I wouldn't want to spend my life working for someone else. But Zeb says he'll make sure I learn enough to be able to start my own shop, doing small engine repairs. That's what I really want. I thought it was impossible, but now you're back. You should take on the responsibility for the farm. You said you would."

"Look, I said I'd talk to Daad about it, but I'm not ready yet." He'd hardly been home long enough for

Daad to have any confidence in him. Maybe he never would.

But Josh didn't seem to be considering that. "When will you be ready?" Josh snapped the question. Obviously he'd expected Ben's homecoming to solve all his problems.

Ben tried to remind himself that Josh was too young to know problems didn't get solved that easily. The weight of expectations on him was starting to feel heavy.

The last time he'd felt that way, he'd run. He wouldn't do that again.

He met his brother's gaze, trying to see past the anger and disappointment there. "After Christmas," he said firmly. "Mamm deserves a happy Christmas without any family quarrels. If you want to bring it up sooner, you'll have to do it yourself."

Josh's face tightened. "You're the one who got me into this. It's up to you to solve it."

Ben's jaw clenched in response. He'd thought Josh was the one person whose acceptance he didn't have to worry about. Looked as if he'd been wrong.

"You boys coming down soon?" Anna called from the bottom of the ladder. "Your *mamm* is saying she should have gone herself instead of sending the two of you to find something."

"We have it," Ben said, leaning over the opening to see Anna's face tilted up to him. "On our way down."

He turned to his brother. "After the holidays," he said firmly. Without waiting for a response, he climbed down the ladder to where Anna waited.

Chapter Seven

Anna collected the broom and dustpan and hurried out of the kitchen before Elizabeth could think of something else she should do. With only two days until Christmas, Elizabeth had launched into a storm of cooking, baking, and cleaning, sweeping Anna along with her. All of their expectant *mammis* were probably doing the same, so they hadn't had any appointments. Anna's thoughts slipped to Dora. She hoped all was going well there, and that the babe would put off its arrival for another week.

Anna scurried into the living room, intent on her current chore, and was surprised to find Ben there, warming himself in front of the propane heater.

"Ach, you surprised me. I didn't hear you *komm* in."

"Shh." Ben's smile flashed. "I slipped in while you and Mamm were occupied."

"Afraid she has a job for you?" she teased.

"Anna, you know me too well. I don't remember Mamm getting in such a tizzy for Christmas in years.

You'd think we were getting ready to host the church for worship."

"She's cleaning everything that stands still, that's for sure." She gestured with the dustpan. "It's a special Christmas, ain't so?"

He didn't pretend not to understand. "I'd hate to think I was the reason for all this extra cleaning. What are you up to? This room is so clean you could eat off the floor already."

"I'm supposed to brush up any needles fallen from the greens on the windowsills." Anna moved to the nearest window and knelt, realizing a short-handled brush would have done the job better.

"It'll just have to be done again on Christmas morning before the rest of the family arrives," he grumbled, but squatted down next to her to help.

"A little extra cleaning is a small price to pay for seeing her so happy." Anna found she was watching his strong, square hand picking up an elusive hemlock needle. "She's so wonderful glad you're home."

His fingers brushed hers. "What about you, Anna?" His voice was low. "Are you glad I'm home?"

She dared to look into his eyes then, her barriers crumbling away like a snowman in the sun. "You know that I am."

Ben clasped her hand, and his was warm and strong. That warmth seemed to flow into her, radiating up her arm and right to her heart. "Anna." He said her name on a breath that caressed her cheek. His fingers tightened. "I…"

"So there you are!" Asa stamped into the room, with Joshua behind him, trying to get a word out.

"Daad, don't." Josh's tone was anguished.

Ben rose to his full height, and Anna scrambled to her feet, still holding the dust pan. "I'm here, ya. What's wrong, Daad?"

"What's wrong is you putting *ferhoodled* ideas in your brother's head."

"Daad, I keep telling you, it's what I want." Josh sent an appealing look to his brother. "It's only Ben returning made it seem possible."

Elizabeth, drawn by all the noise, came in from the kitchen, wiping her hands on her apron. "What is going on here?" she demanded.

"What's going on is Ben encouraging Joshua to turn away from all my plans for him." He glared at Ben. "He's talking about going as an apprentice at the machine shop, of all things."

Elizabeth put a hand on his arm. "Asa, *stoppe*. You know Joshua always used to talk about doing that. If it's what he wants…"

"It's a boy's foolishness." Asa's voice was harsh. "Joshua will have the farm. That's what we decided. That's what's right."

"But I don't want it," Josh burst out. "Ben does."

Anna realized that Ben's hands were clenched into fists so tight that the skin stretched over the knuckles. She longed to reach out and touch him to ease the tension, but she didn't dare.

"You let the other boys choose what they wanted." Ben seemed to make an effort to speak calmly. "Why not Joshua?" His gaze challenged his father, and Anna felt as if the two of them didn't even notice the others in the room.

A flush mottled Asa's cheeks above his beard. "I am offering Joshua a *gut* life running a thriving farm. That's the best any Amish son could have. And the land has needs, too. It needs someone who won't run away from it."

A gasp sounded from Elizabeth. She was on the verge of tears, seeing two that she loved so at odds. Anna's heart hurt for all of them.

Ben was perfectly still. Only the pulse pounding visibly at his temple and the white line around his lips showed his pain.

He took one step toward his father. "Don't make Joshua pay for your disappointment with me, Daad." He spun and stalked out of the house.

Anna imagined she could hear Asa's teeth grinding together. Then he stamped out in the opposite direction. Elizabeth stood there, hands twisted in her apron, seeing her planned Christmas crumbling around her.

Anna shook off her paralysis and hurried to Elizabeth, putting her arms around her.

"I'm so sorry. So sorry," she murmured.

"It's my fault." Josh looked on the edge of tears. "Ben told me to wait until after the holidays. He said he'd go with me to talk to Daad. But I wanted it settled, and Daad was in such a *gut* mood, and I thought... I thought..." He rubbed his face with both hands, not attempting to finish the sentence.

Anna reached out to pat his shoulder. "I'm sorry, too. I wish I could make it right."

"No one can do that," Elizabeth said, straightening. "Asa and Ben must find their own way to each other."

Anna nodded. But in her heart the question echoed. What if they couldn't? Would Ben go away again?

Anna found herself thinking that supper that night was the most miserable meal she'd ever had in this house. Asa ate stolidly, not looking at anything or anyone but his food. Maybe it was best he didn't try to talk. What was there to say that wouldn't lead to an argument?

Joshua, who normally ate everything in sight, picked at his food, pushing it around his plate. Elizabeth barely made a pretense of eating, her gaze drawn again and again to Ben's empty place.

Anna understood, having difficulty keeping her own eyes averted. It seemed impossible to get any food past the lump in her throat, but she was unaccountably thirsty, gulping down her water and pouring another glass.

Finally the meal was over. Asa and Josh left the kitchen without looking at each other. Anna had a sudden desire to shake them. Though even if she did, it probably wouldn't help.

Suppressing a sigh at the stubbornness of men, Anna carried a stack of dishes to the sink and began running hot water. "Let me do the dishes tonight," she said quickly when Elizabeth gestured her away. "You go and rest."

"Resting won't help." Elizabeth's voice was thick with tears. "I must stay busy."

Nodding, Anna moved over and picked up the drying towel. Truthfully, she was the same way. Doing something was the only antidote to being crushed by sorrow. She tried to think of something helpful to say.

"They'll cool off," she finally said. "Give them time."

Elizabeth stared down at the plate she held, but Anna suspected she didn't see it. "What if we don't have time? What if Benjamin is so hurt he leaves again?" She let the plate slide back into the soapy water and turned to grasp Anna's hands. "Talk to him. Please."

Fear swept over Anna at the thought. "But I don't know where he is. Besides, he certain sure won't listen to me."

"Ach, Anna, do you think I don't have eyes in my head?" Elizabeth managed a tiny smile. "You are the one person he might listen to. As for where he is—he'd be where he always went when he was in trouble, with the animals."

When Anna hesitated, Elizabeth squeezed her hands. "Please, Anna."

What could she say? "I'll try. But…"

"That's right. Try." Elizabeth released her. "Go now. Don't let him leave us again."

Even if Ben did talk to her, keeping him from leaving might be beyond her abilities. But she had to try. Getting her coat from the peg, Anna pulled it on and stepped outside, glancing toward the barn.

Darkness was drawing in quickly now that they were in the shortest days of the year. Anna shrugged her coat more closely around her and headed for the barn, not sure whether she hoped Elizabeth was right or not.

But as she slipped into the barn, she saw that Elizabeth did know her son. A battery lantern provided a soft glow, and Ben leaned over the stall gate, patting the pony who was nearly as old as he was.

"Visiting with an old friend?" She tried for a normal tone and feared she didn't quite make it.

Ben acknowledged her presence with a short nod. Not very encouraging, but she moved next to him, reaching over to pat Dolly. The pony whickered and lipped at her hand, searching for a carrot.

"Greedy girl," she murmured. "I don't have anything for you just now."

"There's no point in talking." Ben was abrupt, not looking at her. "Nothing left to say."

"You're wrong there. Joshua has plenty he wants to say. He's so sorry he didn't take your advice he's nearly in tears. He feels he ruined everything."

Ben made a small dismissive gesture. "Probably would have turned out the same either way. It's not Josh's fault. Not Daad's either, for that matter. A couple of weeks at home can't make up for three years away."

The misery in his voice twisted her heart. "Give it time, Ben. Please."

His broad shoulders moved as if to shrug off the idea. "Maybe I never should have come back."

Again she felt the urge to shake someone. "Stop it," she snapped. "Did you think it would be easy? You can't give up at the first little obstacle." Ignoring her own pain, she glared at him.

For an instant Ben glared back, but then his expression eased. "Did I once think you were a quiet little mouse? I was wrong. You're more of a lion."

"Only about some things, like seeing the people I love hurt." She ventured to put her hand on his arm. "Please, Ben. Don't make your family go through that again."

He put his hand over hers, imprisoning her close to him. "What a big heart you have, Anna. You can forgive anyone. Even me."

The warmth of his hand against hers was making it difficult to think. "You didn't do it deliberately. If you found you'd made a mistake about me…"

"Is that what you've been thinking all this time?" He swung around so that their bodies were nearly touching, taking her breath away.

"Isn't that what happened?" Anna found the strength to meet his gaze steadily, even though her heart seemed to be pounding in her ears.

"No." His grip tightened painfully. "Anna, you have to believe me. It wasn't that."

"What was it, then?" If she'd had the breath, she'd have shouted the question. What else could she have thought, finding him gone hours after he'd said he loved her and wanted her to be his wife?

"I was just… I panicked. That's the truth. I thought about what it meant. How we'd get married, have kids, have the same life my parents did. The familiar path. But I'd give up my dreams of seeing the world. I'd never know what it was like out there." He jerked a nod to indicate the Englisch world.

She tried to absorb the idea. Didn't it amount to the same thing? He'd weighed marriage with her against the outside world, and she'd come up the loser.

"Anna," he said her name softly. "I'm sorry. I was an idiot."

"The world out there…was it worth it?"

His jaw tightened. "You know the answer to that, don't you? I came back. This is the life I want. But if it's too late…"

Impulsively she reached up to still the words with her fingers over his lips. "Don't. It's never too late unless you give up."

Something flared in his eyes. He took her hand in his. His lips moved, kissing her fingers, then moving to her palm. Then, his gaze holding hers, he moved his lips to the pulse that beat in her wrist.

Warmth swept her, welling up from deep inside. She couldn't breathe, but she wanted the moment to last forever.

It didn't, of course. But then he stroked her cheek, and followed the trail left by his fingertips with his lips. She swayed toward him even as his arm slid around her and his mouth found hers.

This was no boy's fumbling kiss. It was the kiss of a man who longed for love. All her fears slid away, and she kissed him back with a fire she hadn't known she was capable of.

It might have been a moment or an hour before Ben drew back. She touched her lips, trembling with the joy of being together again.

Ben studied her face as if memorizing it. Finally

he spoke. "Three years ago I wasn't mature enough to know what I had here. Now I am."

Her heart swelled, waiting for him to say the words. To say he loved her, he wanted to marry her.

But he didn't, and the moment passed. Instead he sighed and glanced in the direction of the farmhouse. "Guess I'd better go in and try to make peace. Go with me?"

She nodded, chiding herself for her foolishness. She was as greedy as the mare was, wanting everything at once. She must just be happy to know that his feelings for her hadn't changed. Suppressing the vague edge of disappointment, she focused on her happiness. They would be all right.

Chapter Eight

Making peace wasn't as straightforward as Ben had hoped. Mamm just wanted assurance that he wouldn't leave because of the dispute with his father, and he readily gave it, remembering Anna's tart scolding. Josh was suffering from guilt, angry with himself for precipitating the crisis.

"I didn't mean any harm." He met Ben's gaze with the penitent look he'd worn so often as the mischievous little brother when they were growing up. "I was impatient, and now I've spoiled everything for both of us."

Ben clasped his shoulder with a firm hand, giving him a slight shake. "Quit it. Things work out for the best, ain't so? Now at least Daad knows what you want. Give him time to cool off. I'll talk to him again—try to show him how important this is to you. He doesn't want you to be unhappy."

Josh leaned against the kitchen table and studied his face. "What about you? If I messed it up for you…"

"Don't be *ferhoodled*." Ben managed a smile he

didn't feel. "I messed up my own life, and I can't expect it to be easy to fix." Again he thought of Anna, her cheeks flushed, her eyes snapping. "Whatever happens with me, it will be no more than I deserve. But Daad's always fair. He won't take it out on you once he calms down."

He hoped. Now to attempt to apologize to his father.

But Daad was elusive, busying himself silently with one chore after another. Ben finally got the message. He wasn't talking, not now. Maybe tomorrow. A night's sleep might put this business into better perspective.

When he walked into the dimly lit hallway, he surprised Anna, just starting up the stairs. She stopped, leaning over the banister, concern in every line of her body.

"Did you speak to your *daad*?" she asked, voice soft.

He shook his head, moving closer—close enough to reach out and touch her hand where it rested on the railing. "He's wonderful determined not to talk to me tonight. I'll try again tomorrow." He grimaced. "Christmas Eve. Maybe that will help."

Her fingers closed over his in a gesture of support. "He'll calm down. I know. Your *mamm* will help him see sense."

"Ach, Anna, are you sure you know what you're doing, getting involved with the likes of me?"

"I'm sure." She touched his cheek tentatively, and his heart seemed to leap. He covered her hand with his, pressing her palm against his skin.

Longing swept over him. All he had to do now was speak, and he knew what Anna's answer would be.

They could name the date and put this painful waiting to an end.

No. It wasn't fair. How could he when his future was so unsettled? To say nothing of his past. Until he had something to offer her, he had to wait.

"Good night, sweet Anna." He dropped a kiss on her palm. "Sweet dreams."

A flush rose in her cheeks. "I know what I'll dream of."

Then, as if startled by her own daring, she fled up the stairs.

By the time he rose in the predawn chill, Ben was hoping that Anna's night had been more restful than his. Pulling on his clothes and carrying his boots, he slipped out into the hallway in time to meet Josh emerging from his room, rumpling his hair and yawning.

"Go back to bed," Ben whispered. "I'll do the milking with Daad. It will give us a chance to talk."

Josh nodded. *"Da Herr sei mit du."*

God be with you, Ben repeated silently. That was what he'd been praying throughout the long night…for God to give him another chance to make things right.

When he got downstairs, Ben found that his father had already headed for the barn. Shrugging on his coat, he picked up one of the flashlights that hung next to the door and followed.

It was crisp and cold outside, with the feel of snow in the air. He crunched his way to the barn, his eyes quickly growing accustomed to the darkness.

Daad was already at work milking one of the black-and-white Holsteins. He'd talked sometimes about getting a larger dairy herd, but that would mean putting in milking machines and a cooler so he could sell to a dairy, and he'd never made the move.

"Sleep in, did you, Josh?" His voice was muffled by the cow he leaned against.

"It's not Josh. I told him to sleep in this morning." Grabbing a stool and a bucket, he moved to the next cow. Daad was silent for a moment.

"Think you remember how to do this?" he said finally.

"Worked on a farm out in Illinois for a time. That got me back into the way of it." His stint in Illinois had been when he'd been working his way homeward, even though he hadn't been sure of his intent himself at the time.

He blew on his hands to warm them and began the rhythmic pumping, enjoying the sound of the milk frothing into the pail. Three of the barn cats began circling him, purring loudly, so he squirted milk into a basin for them, smiling at their instant response as they gathered around, lapping it up.

Daad had lapsed into silence…a silence that lasted until they'd nearly finished. If they were going to talk about what had happened the previous day, it was obviously up to Ben to start.

"I wanted to say I'm sorry for arguing with you." He couldn't say he was sorry about his hopes to intercede in Josh's behalf, since that was just what he intended to do.

Daad didn't answer. Because he'd given up on Ben? Or because he was so firmly wedded to his plan for Josh that he wouldn't even discuss it?

"The farm is yours. You'll do whatever you want

with it." Ben pressed down an edge of irritation at his father's silence. "I gave up any claim I might have had when I left, and I'm not asking you to change your mind about me. But I am asking you to give Josh a chance to do what he wants with his life."

"Farming is the best life for an Amish boy," Daad said, repeating the words he'd said so many times before.

"It might be the best life for you and for Daniel and for me, but not for Josh. Like Joseph and his carpentry business, Josh has other plans."

"Someone has to take over the farm. Daniel already has his own place."

"And Joseph has his business. You didn't stop them from doing what they loved." He fought to keep his voice even. It might be too late for him to have what he wanted, but surely not for Josh. "You can give the farm to Daniel's boy, if you want. I'll work it for him until he's old enough to take over. Just give Josh his chance, Daad. Please."

Ben held his breath. There wasn't anything else to say. If it hadn't been enough…

Daad got up, straightening, patting the Holstein absently. "Ach, maybe I was a bit hasty with the boy. I don't want to push him into something that doesn't suit him." He cleared his throat, not looking at Ben. "I'll think on it."

He'd have to be content with that, he supposed, but it was the best he could expect. Daad was deliberate, but he was fair.

"Let's get this milk to the house." Daad picked up two buckets. "If I know your *mamm*, she'll be in a tizzy to get everything ready to go to Daniel's place."

"Right." Holding on to the glimmer of hope, Ben picked up his two pails of milk.

They stepped outside to see the sky growing light in the east. Over the western ridge, clouds gathered thickly. "Looks like snow coming." Ben slid the door shut.

"Wouldn't be surprised." Daad strode along smoothly, not spilling a drop as he went.

They were nearly to the house when Daad spoke again. "So, are you home to stay, Benjamin?"

"Ya, Daad." Home to stay—to go back to the church, make his confession and his vows, commit to live Amish the rest of his life.

But if he was truly to be right with God, he had to deal with his past, and that meant Mickey. Mickey wanted to see him, so the sooner the better. They could meet in town and have this over with once and for all.

From what Anna had been able to observe at the breakfast table, both Ben and his brother looked a bit less stressed. That surely meant that Ben's talk with his *daad* had given them hope.

Any chance of a private word with Ben slid away as Elizabeth sprang up from the table, intent on getting everything ready to head to Daniel's as early as possible. Anna privately thought that Daniel's wife might appreciate a quiet time this morning before the influx of family, but she was swept away inexorably on the wave of Elizabeth's determination.

Ben, stepping out of his mother's path, gave Anna the suggestion of a wink. *Later*, he mouthed silently, and she nodded, reassured.

Later proved to be midmorning, when Elizabeth had hurried upstairs to check over the stack of wrapped gifts in the corner of her bedroom. A peek out the back door showed Anna that Ben was approaching the house. Grabbing her jacket from the peg, she stepped out to wait for him.

Ben increased speed when he saw her, taking the two steps to the porch in one long stride. After a quick glance around to be sure no one was watching, he clasped her hands in his. "How did you get away from Mamm?"

"Shh. She'll be back in a moment." She smiled up at him, convinced the news was good. "Well? Did you talk to your *daad*?"

Ben nodded. "Nothing's sure yet, but I think he's ready to consider Josh's plan. Now, if we can keep Josh from rushing into anything again, it will probably work out for him."

"And you? Will it work out for Benjamin, too?" She clasped his cold hands tighter.

A tiny line formed between his brows. "That's not… well, let's say we'll have to wait and see." He glanced down at their clasped hands. "Funny, that I never realized how much this place meant to me until I came back. Now…well, now I don't know what Daad will decide. I can't blame him for being slow to trust again, can I?"

There was a note of sorrow, maybe even of bitterness, in his words that she didn't miss. But before she could find a response, she heard Elizabeth calling from the kitchen.

Ben released her hands with his teasing grin. "Foiled again. We'd best go in."

Hoping Elizabeth would think her cheeks were red from the cold air, Anna hurried inside, intensely aware of Ben right behind her.

"There you are." Elizabeth looked upset. "I can't believe I did such a foolish thing. How could I?"

"What's wrong?" Anna hurried to her, alarmed.

"Ach, I told Barbie I'd bring the pickles and olives and vegetables for the relish tray, and I went and forgot to pick up the jars of olives when I was at the store."

Anna exchanged glances with Ben, trying to suppress a smile.

"That's a crisis for sure, Mamm." He came to hug her. "Christmas Eve will be ruined if we don't have olives, that's certain sure."

Elizabeth swatted at him. "Don't you go making fun of me, Benjamin. I promised I'd take care of it. Well, we'll have to go to town before we go to Daniel's, I suppose. But that will make us late, and I want to be there to help."

Ben planted a kiss on her cheek. "I'll take care of it. I told Daad I'd do the afternoon milking so he can go early with you. I can easily run into town and get them. How many do you want—two of each?"

Elizabeth reached up to pat his cheek. "Ach, you're a *gut* boy. Better make it three, ain't so?"

Anna could tell by his expression that he thought that was far more than needed, but he was wise enough not to argue. "Right. I'll take care of it and see you at Daniel's later." He hugged her. "And calm down. It's just family, after all."

"Family is the most important after faith," Elizabeth said firmly. "And don't you forget it."

Only the faintest flicker of an eyelash showed that he might have been hurt by the words. "I'll get going," he said. With a quick smile for Anna, he went out the back door.

"He is a *gut* boy," Elizabeth said softly, almost to herself. "Pray Asa sees it."

Anna nodded, not sure Elizabeth even noticed that she was still there.

Elizabeth seemed to shake herself. "Now we'll get everything packed up and…ach, what now?"

Anna hurried to take her cell phone from the shelf. A jumble of words assaulted her ear, so fast she could hardly make it out.

"Slow down, James. I can't understand you. Is Dora all right?"

Apparently Dora wrested the phone from her excited husband. "I… Can I see you, please, Anna? I've had some contractions, and Mamm Beachy says that's natural, but I…"

"I understand," she said quickly, raising her eyebrows at Elizabeth. "I'll *komm* right over. Is anyone else there besides you and James?"

"They already left for Onkel Amos's house. What?" This last was addressed to her husband, apparently. Then she came back on the line. "James says we'll *komm* to the center. That way if everything is all right, we can go on to his *onkel*'s from there." Her voice seemed to tremble. "Please, Anna. I don't know…"

"It's no trouble at all," Anna said reassuringly. "I'll see you at the center."

She clicked off and turned to Elizabeth. "Did you get that? It's probably nothing, but I'll stay and check Dora. You go on to Daniel's."

"I don't want you driving alone when it looks like snow." Distressed, Elizabeth glanced toward the window. "Ach, what am I thinking. Ben will be coming later. Run and catch him before he leaves for town and tell him to pick you up at the center. Hurry, before he leaves." Elizabeth shooed her with both hands.

Knowing it would only stress Elizabeth more if she disputed her plans, Anna picked up her jacket again and dashed out the door.

She spotted Ben by the barn, standing next to the two-seat buggy. There was no need to hurry—he hadn't even brought out the gelding yet. Still, her eagerness for a private word had her feet scurrying across the frozen path to the barn.

It was only when she was within a few feet of him that she realized she was once more catching him unaware, as he talked on his cell phone. Determined not to make the same mistake again, she opened her mouth to given him warning of her presence. But the words froze in her throat when she heard what he was saying.

"...has to be now. I'll meet you in town in about half an hour." The other party must have spoken then because Ben was silent for a moment.

Now she should speak, but she couldn't find the words.

"Mickey, I can't take it any longer. I can't. It has to be today. Meet me. Don't let me down now."

She gasped then, unable to stop herself. It was as if something had smacked her right in the stomach, knocking the breath out of her entirely.

Ben pivoted, clicking off the call. His face tightened until it resembled something formed from the icicles that hung from the barn eaves. "Well, Anna?"

She had to speak, even though she felt her heart splintering. "I was supposed to tell you to pick me up at the birthing center later. But that won't happen, will it? Because you won't be here. You'll be off someplace with that Mickey you were talking to."

A muscle twitched in his jaw, as if out of his control. He started to speak but she swept on, the blood pounding so loudly in her ears she could hardly hear.

"Who is she? Your Englisch girlfriend? How long were you going to pretend that you'd given all that up? How could you pretend about…about us?" She would not cry. Not yet. Not where he could see.

Ben's gaze flashed like lightning. "Made up your mind, haven't you? What happened to trust?"

She forced herself to look full in his face. "Trust is earned, Benjamin. I learned three years ago I couldn't trust you. I shouldn't have forgotten that so easily." Unable to hang on to her composure for another instant, she spun and hurried toward the house.

It had happened again. She had given Ben her heart, and he had broken it. The first flakes of snow, drifting down from a sullen sky, felt like tears on her cheeks.

Chapter Nine

Somehow Anna managed to control herself until after she'd seen Elizabeth, Asa and Josh off to Daniel's house. By then the need to weep or rage had passed, leaving her with a dry throat and stinging eyes.

She got her bag, checking to make sure she had everything she needed. Maybe she wouldn't make it to Daniel's at all for Christmas Eve. If so, that might be just as well. She didn't think she could bear to see joy turn to ashes when they realized Ben had left again.

A very faint flicker of hope touched her. He hadn't actually said he was leaving today. But he'd also said he couldn't stand it any longer. Meaning what? This life? Or her? It would have been better if she'd never seen Benjamin at all.

Pulling on her black gloves, she opened the back door and paused. The snow was falling thicker and faster than she'd realized. It must have accumulated an inch in the past half hour. If this kept up, plenty of people wouldn't get where they'd planned to be for Christmas Eve.

Trudging through the snow toward the birthing center, she felt none of the exhilaration that a fresh snowfall usually brought. Now she could only see it as a hazard.

When she reached the small building, Anna stamped the snow off her sturdy shoes and hurried to turn the heat up. The gas furnace came on with a reassuring murmur. Grateful for the blast of warmth, she stripped off her gloves and hung her outer garments up to dry. At least she didn't have to worry about the heat or light going off if the power lines went down, the way some of their Englisch neighbors would.

Anna bustled around, getting the room ready, checking the supply of sheets and towels for no reason at all except to keep her mind occupied.

It didn't help. She was still mentally following Ben on his way to the village of Lost Creek, the gelding clopping along through the snow.

Or would he have taken the car, which had been tucked away out of sight in one of the outbuildings since he'd returned? If he didn't intend to come back...

But no, surely she'd have noticed the sound of a car. She glanced at the businesslike watch every midwife needed. Would he be meeting his friend yet?

Friend. Girlfriend? Or more?

No point in torturing herself this way. Besides, that was the sound of a buggy drawing up to the hitching rail in front of the clinic.

Swinging her black shawl around her shoulders, she stepped out to greet them and frowned. The snow had been coming down fast a few minutes ago. Now it turned the ridge completely invisible, and when she looked down the valley she could no longer see the lights from the distant Englisch farms and houses.

Planting a smile on her face, Anna went to help James bring Dora up the steps. Reassurance was the first task of the midwife, especially in a situation like this one. "I'm wonderful glad you got here with the snow getting so bad."

James cast a worried look back up the lane toward the road. "Nasty out, that's certain sure."

"Let's get Dora inside where it's warm and see what's happening." She smiled at Dora, seeing the fright in the girl's face. "Here we go."

Together they took her through the waiting room and into the exam room. James, after one nervous glance around, backed out to the waiting room instead.

"There now, if James isn't a typical first-time *daadi*." She assisted Dora to remove her outer clothes and get onto the bed that they used in preference to a more formal exam table.

"I'm *sehr* glad to see you." Dora clasped her hand. "Mamm Etta kept saying these feelings are just practice for the big day, but I can't help being worried. If the baby comes this early—"

"Now, Dora, this wouldn't be early at all. Remember what we told you. Two weeks either way is all right. Now just let me take a look, and we'll soon know."

It didn't take more than a few minutes to know what she was dealing with. Dora was indeed in labor, with the contractions stronger and closer together than she liked to see given the situation. Still, babies arrived when they were ready, snow or no snow.

"James," she called. "Will you *komm*, please?"

James's face was nearly as white as the sheet on the bed, but he came to take Dora's hand. "What...what?" He seemed to run out of words.

Anna focused on their faces, trying to make them feel her assurance. "Dora's right. It looks as if you're going to have your baby for Christmas."

"But...but...it can't be," James protested. "Mamm says the baby won't be born for another week or more."

Anna pushed down a wave of exasperation, but before she could say anything, Dora did.

"This is our baby," she snapped. "Not your *mamm*'s. The baby is coming. I know."

For a moment he looked taken aback. Then he straightened and gave a crisp nod. "Ya. So what do we do?"

"Since the weather is so bad," she spoke carefully, not wanting to alarm them, "it may be best if we call the emergency squad. They should be able to get through. Otherwise, you may be stuck here until the roads are cleared. All right?"

Dora's face crumpled. "But I don't want to go clear to the hospital. I want to have my baby right here, close to home."

"I know," Anna soothed. "That's what we want for you, too." As tears threatened to overcome Dora, she added, "Let's just call and see what they say about getting here, all right? Then we can decide."

Dora hesitated, then nodded.

Anna stepped away from the bed to retrieve her cell

phone. Dora was fine and healthy, and normally there'd be no question of calling anyone to help. But she and Elizabeth were in agreement that they'd call for assistance if any problems arose. She just feared that if she waited, help might not get here in time.

But a glance at the phone took the decision out of her hands. She held up the cell phone to show James. "No service. The weather must be interfering."

James's face tightened. "I'll go myself. The land lines might still be working at one of the farms down the valley."

"No! What if something happened to you? What would I do?" Dora sat up, grabbing his hand, and almost as quickly gasped at the onset of another contraction.

James held her hand in both of his, and Anna seemed to see him turning from an uncertain boy into a man in that moment.

"Hush, now. Nothing will happen to me. It's my job to take care of you and the *boppli*, ain't so? You just listen to Anna, and I'll be back with help before you know it."

Anna nodded. "Take care, now. And be sure to tell the emergency people that it's a first baby and I requested assistance because we might be cut off by the snow." She walked to the door with him as he bundled up against the cold. "God be with you."

James's young face was resolute. "I'll get help. Just… just take care of my Dora." Not waiting for a response, he plunged out into the snow.

Anna let out a long breath. The decision was made.

She could only pray that it was the right one and that God would guide her every action this night.

As Anna might have predicted, James's departure sent Dora into a fit of anxiety. She moved restlessly, unable to be still.

"Something will happen to James. I know it will. Or the baby. What if something goes wrong with the baby?" she wailed.

Anna clasped both her hands, forcing her to listen. "*Stoppe*. You are tiring yourself out, and that won't help you or the baby. When the time comes, you have to be strong enough to push. The best thing now is for you to rest a bit between contractions."

"I can't." Dora tried to pull away.

"Ya, you can," she said firmly. Ordinarily she'd encourage walking at this stage, but calming Dora took priority at the moment. "Lean back against the pillow now, and just listen."

Somewhat to her surprise, Dora obeyed, her anxious gaze fixed on Anna's face. With another silent prayer for guidance, Anna began to talk. She kept her voice low and soothing, focusing all her love and attention on the frightened girl. She talked about the baby, about the joy he or she would bring into their lives. She encouraged Dora to tell her about James's courtship. Slowly, by tiny degrees, the tension drained out of Dora. Relaxing, she stopped fighting her body, resting and letting Anna coach her through the contractions.

Eventually Dora fell into a light doze. Anna stood, stretching. She tiptoed to the window and peered out, but she couldn't see a thing. Except that the snow was still falling, steadily cushioning the world, enveloping it in stillness.

Not so still, she realized suddenly. Someone was moving on the porch. Could James have gotten back already? She hurried to the door.

It opened before she reached it to admit a snow-covered figure. Stamping and brushing off snow, he turned.

"Ben! What are you doing here?"

Heedless of her question, he shed his gloves and grasped her hands. "Are you all right? When I heard you were out here by yourself…"

Irrational joy swept over Anna. Ben was here. What-ever he might intend to do in the future, he'd come back now out of concern for her.

"I'm fine." She glanced toward the other room. "Dora Beachy is here. The baby's coming, and James went to try and get through to the rescue squad. Is that how you knew?"

Ben shook his head. "When I saw how bad it was getting, I checked with Daniel to see if everyone had gotten there. They had—everyone but you. So I came."

He said it so simply, as if there had been no question of any other choice.

"But how? It's so bad out." She helped him shed the heavy, soaked jacket.

"Made it as far as Thompson's place with the horse and buggy, but the drifts were getting too bad. I left the horse there. They'd have brought me on the snowmobile, but Frank Thompson had already taken it to get James to someplace where he could call the rescue squad."

"James is all right, then. Thank the *gut* Lord. But how could you walk in this snow?" Her heart shuddered at the thought of him trudging through the blinding snow and darkness. "You could have been lost..." Her throat closed on a sob.

"Not a chance. Once I saw your light I just kept walking toward it." He took her hands again, holding them securely in his. "Toward you."

Anna's heart seemed to swell. He had come to her. Their foolish quarrel hadn't been the end. She didn't even need an explanation for that phone call. She just needed to know that he'd put her first.

"Anna, I have to tell you..." He broke off at a voice from the other room.

"Anna? Is that James? Is he safe?"

With an effort, Anna drew her hands from his clasp and hurried to Dora. "It's not James, it's Ben. But he says James is fine. One of the Thompson boys took him on their snowmobile to get help."

Dora's face brightened. "I knew he'd get through. My James can do anything he sets his mind to."

"That's right." Anna checked her deftly and listened to the baby's heartbeat. "Nice and strong," she said in answer to Dora's anxious gaze.

Dora's eyes widened as a new contraction began. For an instant she lost focus, and Anna recalled her gently, coaching her through it.

"The baby is getting serious," Anna said, smoothing Dora's hair back from her face. "We have some work ahead of us, ain't so?"

Dora managed a smile for the first time since she'd arrived. "Guess so."

"Anna?" Ben ventured far enough to lean in the open doorway. "Anything I can do to help?" He sounded as if he hoped she would say no.

"Start some water heating in the kettle," she instructed. "I may want to brew some herbal tea. And then you can put a blanket to warm in front of the heater." She gave him a reassuring smile. "Don't worry. I won't ask you to catch the baby. That's my job."

Even Dora chuckled at his expression, but then she took on that listening expression Anna had seen so often before in expectant *mammis*. It was as if what was happening inside their bodies was miles more important than anything outside.

A pang of envy went through her with the longing to experience it herself, but this time it was mixed with just a little hope. Maybe, one day…

Ben had more than one opportunity in the next hour to think that he might be better off out in the snow. But then he'd look at Anna and know how foolish that was. He was here, with her. And if he could help her in any way, he'd happily fetch and carry and try to keep his mind off what she was doing.

Ben tried telling himself that this was like watching a calf or a lamb or any other creature coming into the world. It didn't seem to help much.

Focus on helping Anna, he ordered himself. *That's all you can do now.*

Time ran into itself. Was the night lasting forever,

or was it moving at incredible speed? Dora's small face was beaded with sweat, and he wiped it with a towel without being asked. She shot him a thankful look before returning to that fierce concentration that seemed to shut out everything else.

"We're getting close," Anna said, her tone still invincibly cheerful. "Dora, I want you to hold on to Ben's hands. Pull against them as hard as you can when you feel the urge. Don't worry. You won't hurt him."

Dora nodded and grabbed him, fingers clenching so that he felt them bite into his palms. He hung on and looked to Anna for reassurance.

"She won't mind my being here?" he asked quietly.

Anna smiled, shaking her head. "She's too busy to notice who's here, as long as she has someone to hang on to."

She seemed to be right. Dora accepted him almost without seeing him as she put all her strength into a push.

"Great, Dora. Just great. Here's the baby's head." Anna was focused, her hands deft and strong. "One more push now."

Somehow, Ben wasn't sure how, Dora mustered the strength for another push.

"Easy, breathe now, the way I showed you. Don't push for a moment." Anna sounded calm, but somehow he sensed something was happening.

Dora did, as well. "What's wrong? Is something wrong with my baby?"

"Nothing at all," Anna soothed. "I'm just turning him or her a tiny bit to make it easier, that's all."

He kept his gaze on his Anna's face as he sent up a silent prayer. *Please, God...*

"All right. Just one more push now."

One more, and he couldn't keep himself from looking just in time to see the baby slide out into Anna's hands. For a long moment there was silence, and then an outraged cry sounded lustily. Dora was crying, too, and smiling as well, and it was all he could do to blink back tears himself.

Anna brought the squalling little being to Dora, putting it gently on her chest. "It's a girl. You have a fine, strong baby girl."

Dora's arms circled her child, her face transformed.

His eyes met Anna's across the width of the bed and her face was transformed as well. "We did it," she murmured. "*Denke*, Ben."

He shook his head. "Not me. You did it all."

Funny. He'd grown up knowing that his mother was a midwife, but he'd never really appreciated it until now.

Chapter Ten

It was nearly an hour before Anna had both *mammi* and baby settled. She slipped quietly into the adjoining room, leaving the door open to hear the slightest sound. Ben was leaning back in a desk chair, feet propped on a pulled-out drawer, his eyes closed. She moved a little nearer, a wave of tenderness sweeping over her. He must be exhausted after battling his way through the storm and then helping her deliver a baby. She should let him sleep.

Before she could move away, Ben reached out and caught her wrist, his eyes opening. "*Komm*, sit," he said. "I've been keeping the kettle hot for you." He rose and pushed her gently into a chair. "I'll bring you some tea."

She would argue, but the chair seemed to welcome her, making her realize how tired she was. When Ben brought the tea, she wrapped her hands around the mug thankfully.

"How are they?" He nodded toward the bed.

"Just fine. Both sleeping." Anna stretched her back

and then took a thirsty gulp from her mug. "Is it still snowing outside?"

"Slacking off a bit at the moment, but I'd guess this snowfall will go in the record books," he said, settling into the chair he pulled up next to hers. "No signal on the cell phone yet."

"It's a shame we can't let James know everything's all right. He'll be worried." She pushed back a strand of hair that had come free, wondering how disheveled she looked after the long hours.

"Worried," Ben echoed. He captured her hand in his. "Like I was."

Anna's cheeks flushed. "You shouldn't have risked so much to get here."

"I had to." He moved his fingers on the back of her hand, sending warmth through her. "I had to tell you I was sorry for the way I spoke."

"Ach, no." How could he think that? "I'm the one to be sorry. I didn't trust you. I didn't let you explain." Her voice grew husky on the words as her throat tightened. In response, Ben lifted her hand and kissed her wrist just where her pulse beat heavily.

"Not your fault. Mine. I was the one who was too proud to explain." He shook his head. "Stupid. I should have known I could tell you anything."

"You can," she said, feeling her way, "but you don't have to." She realized quite suddenly that she could say the important words without doubt. "I trust you."

He sent her a questioning glance, seeming relieved at what he read in her face. "It's not surprising that you didn't feel you could, after the way I ran out on you."

"Hush." She put her fingers over his mouth. "You told me about it. I understand."

"I told you why I left. I didn't tell you what happened out there." A nod of his head indicated the outside world. "I didn't tell you who Mickey is."

"You don't have to…" she began.

"I want to." Ben actually looked surprised at himself. "I never thought to tell a soul, but I want you to know."

She had to clear her throat before she could get the words out. "Tell me, then." She wouldn't judge him. Whatever it was, she would understand.

"Mickey was an Englisch kid I got to know when I was a teenager. His family lived in that fancy development over on the other side of Lost Creek."

"He?" Anna said involuntarily.

"Ya, a guy," he said, smiling a little at her relief. "We always talked about hitching our way across the country together, seeing the world. Nothing ever came of it, though. And then that summer three years ago he was back in town, and we got together. Seemed his father wanted him to go on to graduate school, become a lawyer like his *daad* was. Mickey felt like life was getting away from him, and he hadn't done all the things he'd planned. As if his future was all planned out for him."

"The way you felt that last night," Anna said softly, pushing away her own pain at the memory.

He nodded, and she could read the shame in his face. "So you can guess the rest. We took off, making our way west, just bumming around and seeing what we wanted. Mickey had a car and money, and it seemed like we were free."

He stopped, as if not sure how to go on, and Anna knew he had come to the difficult thing—the thing he'd been hiding all along.

"Then something went wrong," she said. "What was it?"

He gripped her hand as tightly as Dora had gripped his when the baby was coming. "It was stupid, I guess. Mickey thought a guy at a store where we stopped had ripped him off. He was steamed about it. He told me to wait in the car for him, and he went back. He said he was just going to tell the guy off. Instead he took the money he figured was owed him."

Anna couldn't suppress a gasp. "He stole?"

"He didn't see it that way," Ben said grimly. "But the police did. Both of us ended up in jail."

"Ach, Ben, I'm so sorry." Her fingers caressed his cheek, hoping she could smooth away the tension. "But *you* didn't do anything wrong."

"No. But…" His face showed the pain that had him in its hold. "We were supposed to go before the judge, and Mickey panicked. All he could think was what his father would do when he found out. If he was convicted that would destroy his chances of ever being a lawyer, and all of a sudden, when he thought he couldn't have it, he knew how much it meant to him." He pressed her hand against his cheek. "Like me, when I came back and realized the farm would never belong to me."

"He wanted you to take the blame." Anna figured it out without his saying it, and her heart ached for him.

He nodded. "Stupid, I guess. But at the time…well, it seemed like I was losing everything anyway, so what difference did it make? Mickey was convinced it would just mean a fine. He'd pay that, and we could walk away."

"It didn't happen like that?" Her heart seemed to be breaking for him.

"The judge sentenced me to seven months in the county jail." He said the words flatly. "Mickey paid the costs. He wanted to give me money, too, but I didn't want it."

"No, you wouldn't." She sought for the words he needed to hear. "It must have been so terrible for you. How could you stand it, being locked up for something you didn't do?"

Ben's mouth twisted. "It was no picnic. Some days I thought I'd go crazy with wanting to walk through a field instead of a concrete exercise yard. But I made it. I had to."

"Why, Ben? Why didn't you come home after you got out of jail?" The words burst out of her.

He shrugged. "Too stubborn. Too proud. I didn't want to admit what a fool I'd been. I thought I wouldn't be welcome. It took me all this time to swallow my pride and admit what I really wanted was to be home again."

For the first time she truly realized why the church considered pride such a sin. It separated you from those who loved you, including God.

"You are home now. That's what counts." She held his hands in both of hers, longing to make him believe her words. "This fuss with your *daad* will settle down. I'm sure of it."

She hesitated, but there was one more thing he probably needed to say. "About those calls from Mickey…"

Ben grimaced. "Maybe he's grown up a bit, like I have. He feels like he owes me something. He wanted to ask my forgiveness." For a moment he was quiet, and she longed to know what he was thinking. "I finally saw that if I was going to come back to my life here, I needed to see Mickey. I couldn't go back to the church without settling my anger with him." He looked into Anna's eyes. "I couldn't ask you to marry me until I'd settled the unfinished business of the past. I had to tell him I forgave him."

Relief swept through her. "And have you?"

"I have." Her heart seemed to heal again at his expression. "Anna Zook, I asked you once to marry me. Now I'm asking you again. Will you marry me?"

A smile teased at her lips. "I only needed once, Benjamin. Ya, I will marry you."

Ben stood, drawing Anna up with him, and pulled her into his arms, and she felt that she, too, had come home.

Several very satisfying kisses later he pulled back just enough to see her face. "I wish I knew what I had to offer you, my Anna. If I'm not to have the farm, I'll have to look for something else."

"It doesn't matter." She was strong in the confidence of his love. "Whatever the future brings, we will handle it. We'll build a life together whether it's here or somewhere else."

He grinned. "Just promise me I won't have to see any more babies being born."

"Only our own," she said, her cheeks flushing. "You won't mind that, will you?"

He drew her close against him, and she longed for the day they would be truly one. "No, I won't mind," he said.

They were still standing close together when the first rays of the rising sun crept over the ridge and brightened the eastern sky. A moment later they heard the roar of a snowplow.

With his hand clasping hers, Ben peered out the front window. "A snowplow, an EMT truck and a police car. It looks like help has arrived in force." He squeezed her hand. "You'll have to tell them that you did fine without their help."

Heart lifting, Anna smiled. "I *had* help." *Thank You, Lord.*

The day after Christmas was known in the Amish world as Second Christmas, a day for visiting with friends and relatives and rejoicing together. As far as Anna could tell, everyone seemed to know already about her and Ben. No one actually said anything, but the knowing glances and frequent smiles gave the secret away.

A steady stream of people had been braving the snowy roads to stop at the house, and Elizabeth was in her element, pressing food and drink on all of them.

As she headed for the kitchen yet again, Anna intercepted her. "You've been on your feet all day. Let me put more coffee on or set out cookies or whatever it was you intended to do."

Elizabeth surprised her with a hug. "I'm so wonderful happy today that I could go on forever, I think." She glanced around to be sure that no one could hear them. "Asa wants to tell Ben himself, but I can't keep it from you, not now. Asa says that with you taking over more of the midwife practice and Ben here to take over the farm, come spring we'll get started on building a *daadi haus* next to this one."

The first thing that registered with Anna was what she'd said about Ben. "You mean it? The farm will go to Ben?"

Elizabeth gave the quick nod that was so typical of her when she was pleased. "Asa sees that Josh is so determined that there's no dissuading him from the job he wants. And he says he's not so *ferhoodled* that he can't see Ben is here to stay now." She squeezed Anna again. "It is just what I always hoped would happen. No one could have given me a happier Christmas. Now you go and visit with folks. I don't need any help just now."

What she wanted to do was to give Ben the good news, but mindful that Asa wanted to do it himself, she contained herself. Still, she maybe should stay clear of Ben for a bit or she'd let the secret out for sure.

A bustle at the door announced the arrival of more visitors, coming in on a tide of cold air and cheerful chatter. Anna blinked at the sight of Etta Beachy and her husband. They were not usual Second Christmas visitors, being neither neighbors nor relatives.

Anna took a step backward. She hadn't seen Etta since the birth of Dora's baby, and she wasn't sure she wanted to encounter her now. Another stealthy step, and she backed right into Ben's strong figure. He steadied her with a hand on her elbow and leaned close to whisper in her ear.

"You're not looking for a place to hide, are you?" he murmured. "After all, this is your home. Our home, in fact."

She spun to meet his gaze. "Your *daad* told you?"

His eyes danced. "Ya. And I see Mamm couldn't resist telling you, ain't so? Have you seen how happy Josh is looking?"

"He'll be as happy as we are." The joy that bubbled up in her just had to be shared.

Ben shook his head. "He couldn't possibly be as happy as I am right now. And you…"

He was interrupted by a rush of movement behind her. The next instant Anna was enveloped in an enormous hug. "Ach, Anna Zook, you are just the person I wanted to see. Our little granddaughter is doing fine, thanks to you, and she's the prettiest newborn I ever saw in my life." Etta's ruddy face beamed with pleasure. "I always said you are a wonderful fine midwife."

Anna heard a chuckle behind her and felt sure that Ben was on the verge of saying something she'd rather he didn't. She gave him a quick nudge with her elbow, not daring to meet his eyes.

"I'm glad they're doing so well. Will they be home soon?"

"Tomorrow, the doctor at the hospital says. Not that we needed him, but with the weather so bad, it was best to be on the safe side, ain't so?"

It was hard to keep a straight face when Ben was

standing so close and barely containing himself, but she managed. "Tell Dora we'll stop by to see her in a few days."

"Gut, gut." Etta sent a sly glance from her to Ben. "I hear tell we'll be celebrating with the two of you before long, too. You're just what Benjamin needs, ain't so?" Before either of them could say a word, she'd whisked off to greet someone else.

Anna turned to Ben. "Don't you dare laugh at her," she said. "I like her much better this way."

"I wouldn't dream of laughing." He drew her out of the flow of traffic. "I agree with her. You're just what I need." His intent gaze brought a flush to her face. "And the sooner the better."

For an instant she was afraid he'd kiss her right there in front of everyone, but he didn't. "Happy Christmas, Anna," he murmured softly.

"Happy Christmas, Ben." Joy lent wings to her words. This truly was the happiest Christmas she'd ever had, and with God's blessing, she and Ben would have many more to share together.

* * * * *

Dear Reader,

Merry Christmas, and welcome to an Amish Christmas celebration in Lost Creek, Pennsylvania. The Amish don't celebrate Christmas in just the same way as their Englisch neighbors, and sometimes not even in the same way from one Amish settlement to another. The strong prevalence of Pennsylvania German folk traditions affects most of us here in Pennsylvania, including the Amish. What would Christmas be without the Moravian Star or the *putz* (manger scene) or the Christmas pickle? (And if you don't know about the Christmas pickle, you're missing a delightful time as the pickle ornament mysteriously moves from one place to another in the days leading up to Christmas!)

I've written about midwives in several books, and when I was asked to do an Amish Christmas novella, my mind immediately jumped to the idea of writing about an Amish midwife. From there it was a quick progression to thinking about a Christmas snowstorm, an unexpected baby and a story about the forgiveness brought to each of us by the Christmas Child.

I hope you'll enjoy my story. I'm writing it in the aftermath of a joyous Christmas celebration with my own loved ones, and it comes from my heart.

If you'd like to receive a signed bookmark and a copy of my Pennsylvania Dutch recipe brochure, email me at marta@martaperry.com or find me online at www.martaperry.com. And if you prefer to write a letter, send it to me in care of Love Inspired Books, 195 Broadway, 24th Floor, New York, NY 10007. I'll be happy to answer you.

Blessings,

Marta Perry

A CHRISTMAS TO REMEMBER

Jo Ann Brown

For my family
Thanks for keeping the Christmas traditions
we share alive

Can two walk together, except they be agreed?
—*Amos* 3:3

Chapter One

From where he stood in the darkened store, Amos Stoltzfus watched a small hand rising over the edge of the shelf. Tiny fingers inched around one of the loaves of bread on display at the front of Amos's grocery store. They vanished, both the fingers and the bread, and soft footfalls rushed toward the front door.

Pushing away from the counter where he'd been arranging bottles of the honey Hannah Lambright had brought in from her hives earlier, Amos cut down the other aisle. He reached the door as the tiny thief came around the corner by the milk cooler.

The little girl didn't look more than four or five. The top of her head wouldn't reach Amos's waist. Her blond hair was neatly braided, and the *kind*'s clothing appeared to be new. There were no holes visible where her blue dress hung below her wool coat. The toes of her black sneakers were scuffed, but the wear was slight.

Someone took *gut* care of the little girl. So why was she trying to steal a loaf of bread? Occasionally one of the local teens would try on a dare to take something from the store without paying for it, but Amos had learned to recognize the warning signs. The nervous way the kid refused to meet his eyes or how the would-be thief wandered around the store waiting for an opportunity to snatch and flee.

Had someone put this *kind* up to a prank while Amos was closing the store? What a low thing to do!

He glanced out the window, but the parking lot was lost in shadow. Darkness fell early as the first day of winter approached. He couldn't determine if someone was waiting there for the girl.

"Hello, young lady," Amos said.

The *kind* stared at him with big blue eyes as she held the bread behind her back. "Hewwo," the child said with a definite lisp that suggested she was younger than she looked.

"Can I help you?"

"No." She shook her head, sending strands of fine golden hair into her eyes. As she raised a hand to wipe it away, she gasped and stared at the loaf she held.

"Wouldn't you like a bag for the bread?" Amos asked. "It may seem not heavy now, but it'll get heavier each step you take beyond the door."

The girl looked from Amos to the bread. Stuffing it onto the nearest shelf, she ran toward the door.

"Wait," Amos said.

The *kind* halted, a sure sign she was reared in a *gut* home. When she looked at Amos, tears glistened on her cheeks.

His heart threatened to break at the terror on the little girl's face. No *kind* should ever have to display such dismay and fear. "Don't you want some peanut butter to go with your bread?" He smiled at the little girl. "Bread is pretty boring without something on it."

She sniffed and rubbed her knuckles against her nose before wiping away tears.

Collecting the bread and taking a jar of peanut butter off a nearby rack, Amos put them in one of the cloth bags his customers preferred. He held it out to the little girl. "Pay me when you can. If you can't, do something nice for someone else. Our Lord teaches us: *give, and it shall be given unto you.*"

The *kind* regarded him, confused, and Amos knew the little girl was thinking only of getting away.

"Take it," he urged. He must look like a giant to her. Though he wasn't the tallest of the seven Stoltzfus brothers, he towered over the little girl.

"Danki," the *kind* whispered. *"Danki*, mister."

"Amos. My name is Amos." He smiled. "If you want, I've got some silverware. You can make a sandwich for yourself before you leave. You won't be delaying me. I need to finish sweeping up."

The girl shook her head and grabbed the doorknob. Turning it, she threw the door open and fled, the bag slapping her short legs.

Amos was surprised when the little girl sped in front of the doors opening into the rest of the businesses at the Stoltzfus Family Shops, the buggy shop and the woodworking and carpentry shops his brothers ran. He'd expected her to race along the road.

His eyes widened when he saw someone move as the

little girl skidded to a stop. In the faint light from his brother Joshua's buggy shop, a silhouette of a slender woman emerged from the darkness near the hitching rail used by their plain customers. She put her hand on the girl's shoulder.

What was going on?

Amos paused long enough to grab a flashlight from a nearby display. He strode toward the woman and the little girl. He saw the *kind* whirl and point at him, but neither the woman nor the girl spoke. He struggled to tamp down the outrage rising through him at the thought of a grown woman sending a *kind* to do her dirty work.

He aimed the light at the woman. She was dressed plainly. Like the *kind*, she had a dark coat on. Beneath it, she wore a dark cranberry dress. A black bonnet revealed her hair was as blond as her brows. Her eyes were paler than the *kind*'s, but navy ringed the irises.

Pretty. The unbidden thought formed before he could halt it. However, he took it as a warning. His head had been turned by a lovely woman once, turned round and round until he was too dizzy to think straight. He'd offered her his heart, and she'd spurned him. That had been five years ago, but he'd learned his lesson. Only a fool would be taken in by beautiful eyes and the curve of enticing cheekbones.

"Did you send her into my store to steal?" he asked, anger lacing through his question.

"Who are you?" The woman stared at him with candid curiosity.

"Amos Stoltzfus, and that's my store where your young friend was trying to sneak out with a loaf of bread." He spoke more sharply than he should have, and the woman recoiled.

"No! That's wrong!" She looked at the *kind*. "Were you in the store?"

Before the little girl could answer, Amos demanded, "Why are you letting such a little *kind* out of your sight? It's dark, and *Englischers* often drive their vehicles into the parking lot really fast. She could have been hit!"

"I know." She put a hand to her forehead and rubbed it, then winced. "But I don't know."

"What are you talking about?"

The little girl tugged on the woman's coat and lisped, "Winda."

Or that was what Amos thought the *kind* said until the woman met his gaze. "She means Linda. She tells me my name is Linda and hers is Polly."

"Tells you? I don't understand."

"I've got to assume she's right about our names because I don't remember anything before a half hour ago."

Linda struggled to focus her eyes, which blurred each time she blinked. She saw shock on Amos Stoltzfus's shadowed face. That incredulity was something she needed to get used to, because he wouldn't be the only one horrified she couldn't remember her name or the *kind*'s name when she'd come to herself less than an hour ago. Everything before that was lost in a thick fog.

Her memories must exist. She wasn't a newborn *bop-pli*. She had no idea what had happened and why she couldn't remember. Was Polly her daughter or her sister or someone else's *kind*? They must have known each other for a while because the little girl acted comfortable around her.

It might be easier to think if her head didn't ache. The pain centered near her right ear, but swelled across her forehead. Her headache made her eyes lose focus and set everything spinning.

"What happened to you?" Amos asked.

"I wish I could tell you." Every word was a struggle, but some sense she couldn't identify warned she needed to stay awake. She must not allow the pain to suck her down. "I remember walking here and deciding to take a break by the hitching rail. That's it until Polly came with you chasing after her."

She wondered if he understood she hadn't realized the little girl had entered the store. It seemed that one minute, the *kind* had been beside her; then she wasn't. Then she returned with Amos. How long had Polly been gone?

He held out a cloth bag. "Here's some bread and peanut butter. I offered to let her eat in the store while I finish cleaning for the day. You're both welcome to come inside."

"Danki." She glanced toward the road and winced as the motion set off a new tidal wave of pain. She tried to ignore it as she reached for the bag. Her fingers closed inches from it. A groan burst from her lips.

Amos put a strong, steady hand under her elbow as Polly cried out her name. Linda realized she was swaying. She closed her eyes and concentrated on keeping her balance.

What's wrong with me? Lord, help me.

"Are you okay?" she heard Amos ask.

"I will be." She stepped away, taking care not to tumble over her feet. Looking into his brown eyes, she murmured, "*Danki* for the food."

He frowned. "It's going to snow. You can't stay here. Do you have somewhere to go?"

She pondered his question and looked at Polly who was watching with dismay. "I must, but I don't know where."

"We're going to see *Grossmammi* and *Grossdawdi*," Polly said.

Amos hunkered down beside the little girl, and Linda noticed his hair, in the glow from the flashlight, was brown with ruddy streaks. "That sounds like a lot of fun."

"*Ja.*" The little girl nodded so hard Linda had to look away before her eyes unfocused completely.

"You know Linda's name. Do you know the names of your grandparents?"

"*Ja.*" She sounded disgusted that he'd asked such a question.

"*Gut* for you," Amos said with a smile. "I should have known a big girl like you would know. Will you tell me their names?"

"*Ja. Grossmammi* and *Grossdawdi.*" She grinned with pride.

As he stood, Amos's expression didn't change. He kept smiling, and she guessed he didn't want to upset Polly. He must be a nice man. Or was he? She didn't know if she was a good judge of character or not.

Why have I lost everything, Lord? The anguish came from her heart.

"I assume you don't know their names either, Linda," he said.

"No." It was easier to admit than she'd expected. Or maybe she was too tired and achy and lost to pretend.

"You can't stay here overnight. Once the snow starts—"

When he looked past her, she shifted to see snowflakes drifting in an aimless pattern. They melted as soon as they touched the asphalt parking lot, but more followed.

Polly gave an excited yell and whirled about, trying to catch them on her tongue. Joy flowed in her laughter.

Linda smiled faintly. Every change of expression sent pain along her face, but it was impossible not to be captivated by the little girl's happiness.

"That settles it," Amos said as he turned off his flashlight, leaving them in the thick gray twilight. "You two will have to go home with me."

"What?" All inclination to smile vanished. What sort of woman did Amos Stoltzfus think she was? Why would he assume that she'd agree to such an arrangement with a stranger? A sob caught in her throat. She was a stranger to *herself*, too.

He held up his hands as if to keep her dismay at bay. "Before I offered the invitation, I should have told you that I live with my *mamm* and some of my brothers." He pointed to the doors of the other shops. "My brothers own these businesses. Our farm is outside the village. There are empty bedrooms since a few of my brothers and sisters have married. You're welcome to stay until…"

She understood what he didn't want to say. *You're welcome to stay until you remember everything.* What if she never did? She'd lost more than her memories. She'd lost herself, everything she was and everything she hoped to be.

"It's snowing, Winda! Isn't it *wunderbaar*?" Polly grasped her hands and nearly jarred Linda off her feet.

Amos's hand on her elbow kept her standing. In not much more than a whisper, because she guessed he didn't want Polly to hear, he said, "She needs to get out of the cold."

"Ja." Linda edged away from Amos's fingers which sent a sensation through her that was *not* cold. How could she be drawn to him now?

"*Komm* in while I finish. After that, we'll head to my family's house."

What choice did she have? Even if she could remember where she and the *kind* were bound, she didn't know how they'd get there on a snowy night.

Calling to Polly to join them, Linda looked at the tall man whose face she couldn't see clearly. "Can I ask you a question, Amos?"

"Ja. Ask as many as you wish."

"Where are we?"

His voice was gentle as he replied, "Paradise Springs in Lancaster County in Pennsylvania. That's near—"

"I know where Lancaster County is."

"You do?"

She gave him a weak smile. "Somehow I know

things like that, but don't know anything about my-self. Strange, isn't it?" She hesitated, then asked, "What day is it?"

"Thursday."

"No, I mean what's the date?"

"December 14th."

"Oh." She wasn't sure what else to say. Curiosity had spurred her questions, but she didn't know what to do with the answers.

"Go now?" Polly asked. "I'm cowd."

Linda shivered. She was cold, too.

"And you're hungry, too, Polly, ain't so?" Amos grinned.

"Ja!" The little girl jumped up and down in excite-ment.

"What do you say to some sandwiches to tide us over until supper, Linda?" he asked.

She opened her mouth to answer, but no words emerged. Everything and everyone in front of her rip-pled like a puddle in the rain. The edges of her vision darkened. She thought she heard someone call her name as firm arms kept her from collapsing, but the sound, the arms and the rest of the world vanished into black-ness.

Chapter Two

Linda opened her eyes and stared at a white ceiling. No rafters or water stains broke the painted expanse. A propane lamp hung from the center, its flame turned low. She started to move her head, but pain exploded like a sky filled with fireworks behind her eyes. She squeezed them shut and rode the wave of pain until it eased.

Fireworks...

She remembered fireworks. Maybe from the Fourth of July. Standing by a fence and watching them detonate in the distance. Waiting for the bang to follow almost a minute later. The heat of a humid summer day and the smell of freshly cut grass and a charcoal fire. Hamburgers? *Ja*, but when she tried to recreate more of the scene to see where she stood and who else was there, the fragments of memory vanished as if they'd never existed.

Tears filled her eyes. She refused to let them slip past her lashes to fall down her face. Why was she crying? What filled her mind could have been something she read or someone else had described to her. The tantalizing bits of memory might not be her own. *Focus on the here and now*, she told herself. *Guide me, Lord, until I find my way.*

When she opened her eyes a second time, she looked around. She was in a living room if she were to guess by the furniture. A braided rag rug was on the floor in front of a fireplace. A gas fireplace, she realized when she noted how the fire came from behind the logs rather than within them.

A clock ticked steadily. She hoped it wouldn't chime. That would be agony.

Closer she saw a low table. On top was a bowl filled with water. A cloth hung over its edge, and she realized another damp cloth was draped across her forehead. For a moment, she savored its gentle warmth, letting it sink into her.

"How are you doing, Linda?" asked a woman.

Her eyes struggled to bring the woman sitting beside her into focus. Concern was vivid on the woman's face as she wrung the cloth from the bowl and used it to replace the one on Linda's forehead.

"I don't know," Linda replied as she examined the woman's features, desperate to know her.

Someone else spoke. "Don't try to recognize where you are." The deep voice, though the words were soft, resonated through her. She knew that voice! "You've never been here before, and you've never met my *mamm*, Wanda Stoltzfus, before."

She turned her head on the pillow and fought not to wince. Amos Stoltzfus leaned one shoulder against a staircase. His arms were crossed over his chest, and his face was drawn. She couldn't keep from smiling. Not only was he familiar, but his words were the kindest ones she could imagine.

She *had* been struggling to place this room and the woman. Despite knowing her memories were lost, she'd longed to see something she knew.

Some*one*.

And Amos understood. She appreciated his words more than she could have guessed. He walked toward her, and she was amazed such a tall man was able to walk lightly in work boots.

Tears welled into her eyes at his unspoken kindness, surprising her. Was she usually sentimental, or was weakness causing her eyes to fill? Another question she couldn't answer.

He knelt by the sofa. "My name is—"

"I remember your name." The tears bubbled to the edge of her eyelashes at the words she'd feared she'd never use again. They tasted as sweet as the year's first strawberries. "Amos Stoltzfus. You work at a store."

He smiled. "That's right."

"I was there. With Polly!" She tried to push herself up. "Where's Polly?"

"She's fine." Wanda put a gentle hand on her shoulder. "Amos brought you and Polly here." Wanda smiled, and Linda saw the resemblance between *mamm* and son. Something around the eyes and the way their lips tilted when they grinned. Amusement laced through her voice as she added, "He figured one of us women here would know what to do. My daughter-in-law, Leah, is in the kitchen feeding the *kinder*. Your Polly and her Mandy. Are you hungry?"

She was, but many questions demanded an answer before she ate. She pushed herself to sit up. Amos slid his arm behind her shoulders to assist her. She stiffened as the aroma of his shampoo and soap enveloped her.

"Am I hurting you?" he asked, turning to look at her.

Their faces were so close a *kind*'s hand couldn't have fit between them. She stared at his strong jaw and his expressive mouth that was drawn in a straight line. His dark brown eyes, volatile in the parking lot, were now shadowed with worry.

For her.

Silly tears flooded her eyes at the thought of someone caring about her. She'd been alone, save for Polly, not knowing if anyone wondered where they were. Temptation teased her to rest her head on his shoulder and let his strong arms surround her to hold the world at bay.

But she couldn't. For many reasons, but the primary one was the little girl sliding off a chair in the kitchen and watching her with a troubled expression. Another girl, who looked about ten-years-old and must be Mandy, stared, too.

God, help me find the strength.

Linda drew away from Amos. She murmured her gratitude but settled herself against the back of the sofa. Her head felt too heavy, and she let it drop.

"Ouch!" she gasped, sitting straighter. She was horrified to see strands of hair tumbling forward. It must have fallen out of her bun. Glancing at Amos, she groped for her hair. Where was her *kapp*? No man but her husband should see her hair loose and without a cover.

Her fingers froze. Did she have a husband? She had no idea.

"There's a big lump above your right ear." Wanda tucked Linda's loose hair between her shoulder and the sofa, then grimaced. "I'll get you one of my *kapps*, but I wanted to make sure you don't need stitches."

"Where is my *kapp*?" Its shape could be a clue to where she'd come from or where she was going.

"You weren't wearing one," Amos said.

"But why would—"

The cry of Linda's name in an adorable lisp cut through her words. Polly rushed toward her. Linda tried not to groan when the little girl threw herself against her, saying Linda's name over and over. Wrapping her arms around Polly, Linda held on for dear life. This *kind* needed her. Something horrible had happened to them, and she wasn't going to allow it to happen again. It was a vow she intended to keep...somehow.

Amos watched raw emotions racing across Linda's face, and he realized no matter what had happened to her, she cared for the little girl who clung to her. He'd been heartsick when Linda opened her eyes and looked around like a starving soul seeking God's love. His first thought had been to let her know she was safe.

He'd been shocked when Linda fainted in the parking lot. He'd caught her as he tried to soothe Polly's terror, hoping his reassurances would prove to be true. When he'd put Linda in his buggy and assisted Polly in before locking up the store, he'd prayed Linda would awaken. His prayers hadn't halted during the short drive to the farm where he'd been born and lived his whole life nor had they eased when he carried her into the house, shocking his *mamm* and Leah, his older brother Ezra's wife.

When he'd placed Linda on the couch, he'd followed his *mamm*'s instructions and then stayed out of the way while *Mamm* removed Linda's bonnet and coat. Leah had steered Polly into the kitchen when the unmistakable color of blood was revealed on Linda's bonnet.

What had happened to her? Had her injury stolen her memories? A quick search of her coat had revealed nothing to identify her. Polly had said they were traveling, so he assumed Linda had been carrying a purse. Where was it? He guessed she didn't know. Otherwise, she would have seen her name on the ID insert in her wallet. If she'd filled it out. He had no idea if she was organized or not. As his siblings often reminded him, not everyone was as conscientious as he was. He ignored them, because not being careful had led to being made a fool of by Arlene Barkman five years ago.

Polly rubbed tears off her chubby cheeks as she leaned her head against Linda's shoulder. He watched them and was surprised when Leah spoke close to him. He hadn't noticed her coming to stand beside him.

Her voice was a whisper. "Polly loves Linda. I wonder how they're related."

"That should be easy to answer," he answered before he raised his voice to ask, "Polly, is Linda your *mamm*?"

The little girl looked at him as if he'd grown a second head. "No!" In the lisp, he found easier to decipher each time the *kind* spoke, Polly went on, "She's Linda. My Linda. Not my *mamm*."

"Linda is her name. What's your *mamm*'s name?"

She gave him the same incredulous look she had in the parking lot. "*Mamm*'s name is *Mamm*."

"Ask a silly question," murmured his own *mamm*, and his sister-in-law struggled to hide a smile.

Linda gave him a sympathetic glance, which he appreciated. He was spared from trying to devise something to say when he heard a knock. He went to the door and opened it, knowing who was there.

"*Komm* in, Dr. Montgomery," he said, stepping aside to let the tall, slender redhead enter. The *Englisch doktorfraa* was dressed in a navy coat, a skirt of the same color and an unadorned white blouse.

"Thank you, Amos," she said with a calm smile. "I assume my patient is in the front room."

"*Ja. Mamm* is watching over her."

"Then she's in good hands."

"The best."

The *doktorfraa* slipped off her coat after setting her black bag on the stairs. Picking up the bag, she walked past him.

Amos went into the kitchen when, after introducing herself to Linda, Dr. Montgomery suggested she'd like privacy to examine her patient. When his *mamm* joined him in the kitchen while Leah returned to washing the dishes, Polly came with her. The littler girl had question after question until *Mamm* distracted both *kinder* with cookies.

His own curiosity couldn't be deflected so easily. He glanced into the other room. As he watched, Linda touched her right forefinger, then her left one to her nose. Following the *doktorfraa*'s orders, she reached to do the same to Dr. Montgomery. She paused and looked past the *doktorfraa* when a giggle came from the kitchen and Polly asked if she could play, too.

When Linda caught him staring, he expected her to look away. He expected *himself* to look away. Neither of them did as, for a breathless moment, his gaze entwined with hers. For that second, he sensed the frustration and panic boiling inside her. An urge to put his arm around her and hold her close until the fear subsided shocked him. He didn't know her or anything about her, yet he couldn't deny the unexpected longing crashing over him.

Stop it! he told himself. He'd been fooled by one pretty woman when he discovered he hadn't known enough about her. He wouldn't do that again.

Dr. Montgomery closed her bag and sighed, breaking the connection between him and Linda. "All I can tell you is that you were struck above your ear, and you've suffered a concussion which is the most likely cause of your amnesia."

"There isn't anything you can do to help?" Amos asked, walking into the front room.

"Other than prescribing two acetaminophen tablets every six hours for pain, there's nothing I can do but order some neurological tests and scans. I'll contact Dr. Vandross, the chief neurologist at the hospital, and get his advice to see if we need to arrange some tests and scans."

Linda started to shake her head, then holding it in her hands said, "I don't have any money, and I can't ask this district to pay for a stranger's medical bills."

Mamm sat beside Linda on the sofa. "Don't fret about such things. It'll take a while before the tests can be scheduled." She raised her eyes to Dr. Montgomery. "Isn't that right? When Leah's *daed* needed tests last year, it took some time to fit him into the schedule."

"The full battery of tests might happen before Christmas, but more likely afterwards." The doctor gave Linda an apologetic smile. "I know it must be frustrating to lose your memories, but having the tests won't guarantee their return. Time is the best healer. It's important you don't bump your head until your brain has a chance to heal. Another trauma to your skull and your brain could be damaged worse."

"And keep my memories from coming back?"

"That's one possibility. Another possibility is that you'd suffer injuries leaving you unable to do physical things or talk."

Her eyes grew round with unabashed horror. "That could happen if I bump my head again?"

"I can't say what might happen or not happen. We know too little about the brain and how it handles an injury. If you feel dizzy, sit immediately. Don't take chances." She smiled sadly. "I don't want to scare you, but being careful is vital."

"We understand," Amos said when Linda didn't reply.

"I'd like to see Linda in my office after Christmas if she's still in pain. Can that be arranged?"

"Ja," said Amos.

"If she regains her memories—even bits of them— let me know. What she recalls may help determine what we do next."

"Danki, Dr. Montgomery," he added as he stepped aside to let *Mamm* walk the *doktorfraa* to the door. He guessed his *mamm* had other questions she wanted to ask without Linda overhearing.

If she got answers, Amos saw no sign of it when *Mamm* bustled into the living room and insisted Linda eat. Linda took the bowl of stew, setting it on the table in front of the sofa. She didn't touch it after his brother Ezra came inside when the barn chores were done. His other unmarried brothers returned home from work to eat their supper. The stew grew cold after Polly gave Linda a kiss good-night before Leah took her and Mandy upstairs to bed. *Mamm* refilled the bowl with warm stew before going through the connecting door to the *dawdi haus*, but Linda didn't taste it. When Leah and Ezra asked if she wanted help to go into the guest room beyond the kitchen, she thanked them and sat with her hands folded on her lap.

Amos said nothing as he sat in a chair near the couch and stared at the flames leaping in the gas fireplace. It, along with the old woodstove in the kitchen, kept the whole house warm except on the coldest days of the winter. He unlaced his work boots, then he toed off one and then the other.

"You know *Mamm* is going to be disappointed if you

don't eat," he said as he glanced over at Linda, half expecting her to be asleep.

"Moving makes me dizzy," she said in little more
than a whisper.

"Do you want me to spoon it for you?"

He was so sure she'd say no he almost gasped aloud
when she said, "*Ja*. I don't want to spill anything on
the couch."

That she was thinking of others when she was suffering no longer surprised him. He'd seen how worried
she was about Polly.

"Do you mind?" He pointed to the cushion beside
her.

"Gently, if you don't mind."

He tried not to shift the cushion, but he must have because she closed her eyes and her breath caught. "Once
you have something in your stomach, you should take
some Tylenol."

"That's a *gut* idea."

He picked up the bowl and the napkin. He handed
her the latter and couldn't help smiling when she tucked
it into the top of her dress.

She smiled in return. "If I'm going to be fed like a
boppli, I should dress like one, ain't so?"

Instead of answering, he lifted a spoonful of his
mamm's fragrant stew and held it out for her to eat. He
couldn't think of Linda as a *boppli*. She was a grown
woman, something he was too aware of when she gazed
at him as the tip of her tongue chased a bit of gravy
from the corner of her mouth. He looked at the bowl

he held. He needed to keep his mind on his task and not on her lips.

When the last bit of stew was gone, she handed him the napkin and thanked him. He took the bowl to the kitchen. Leaving it in the sink, he got two tablets from the downstairs bathroom, and returned to the living room with them and a glass of water.

"If you want," he said as she swallowed Tylenol, "I can help you to the guest room."

"No," she replied, staring at the fire. "I shouldn't sleep. It's dangerous after a head injury."

"Did the *doktorfraa* mention that?"

"I remember someone saying that." She closed her eyes and sighed. "But not who. What do I do now?"

"Prayer always helps me. Turning my problems over to God."

She smiled sadly as she looked at him. "Trust me. I'm praying as hard as I know how."

"Then believe God sees everything."

"I wish He'd share a little bit of what He's seen lately with me."

He smiled in spite of himself. "*Mamm* always says a *gut* attitude helps in any situation."

"Even this one?"

"Why not give it a try? Maybe it'll work." *And then you can return to your life, and I can do the same.* He was contrite immediately, though he knew how Linda could mess up his well-organized life. He wasn't going to let a pretty woman do that again.

Chapter Three

Amos came down the stairs the next morning. He'd gone up to change into clean clothes because he didn't want to go to the store in what he'd worn all night. He'd stayed awake, making sure Linda did the same. It'd been tempting to close his eyes and drift to sleep, but he'd seen her fear when she asked him to help her to evade sleep.

He stifled a yawn as he walked into the kitchen, glad Leah had made the *kaffi* extra-strong this morning. His brothers and bleary-eyed Mandy were at the table, eating. With everyone having different schedules, they seldom ate together at breakfast. He listened as Micah and Daniel, the twins, debated some aspect of carpentry. They were working for an *Englischer* contractor to the east in Chester County.

Nodding to them and Jeremiah, who looked as exhausted as Amos felt, he went to the counter to pour himself a mug of *kaffi*. Ezra wasn't in from barn chores, and *Mamm* was helping Leah prepare breakfast as conversations swirled around the kitchen.

It became silent. He turned to see Linda walking in from the guest room. She held Polly's hand, and she faltered when every eye turned in her direction. A hint of color in her face suggested she was feeling better in spite of a sleepless night. Her hair was covered by one of *Mamm*'s heart-shaped *kapps*.

The now familiar yearning to protect her surged through him, and he was on his feet before he realized he was moving. He strode across the room, giving her what he hoped was a bolstering grin. "Sit anywhere you'd like and grab what you can before my brothers eat everything in sight."

She smiled faintly while his brothers protested they'd left enough for her and the *kind*. When he put a steadying hand on her arm to make sure she didn't trip on the rag rugs scattered around the pale blue kitchen, she didn't pull away. He kept his steps short so she and Polly could match them.

Once Linda and the little girl were seated, Polly choosing a chair beside Mandy, he pointed to each of his brothers and told her their names. He sat across from her, and, after joining her and the *kind* in bowing their heads for grace, passed the steaming dishes of food. He frowned when Linda took a single spoonful of scrambled eggs and one slice of toast.

"Don't you want more?" asked *Mamm* as she sat.

"As unsteady as my stomach is," Linda said, "I'm not sure how much I can eat."

"Making haste slowly is always a *gut* choice."

Amos looked at the little girl beside Linda. Though her eyes were as heavy as Mandy's, Polly filled her plate to overflowing. When some fried potatoes fell onto the table, she scooped them up and put them on the plate with a giggle.

He assisted her with putting blackberry jam on her toast, explaining about the person who'd brought the berries into the store to sell the previous summer. Both girls listened, wide-eyed, while he spun a tale about the man noticing how the bushes were shaking. He'd assumed someone else was picking on the other side. The man discovered he was right when he looked over the bush to see a bear gorging itself on the juicy berries.

"What did he do?" Polly asked.

"The bear kept picking and eating."

"What about the man?" asked Mandy, just as excited.

Amos smiled. "He found another patch of blackberries to pick in."

The girls giggled. His brothers guffawed, though they'd heard the story before, and Linda gave him another feeble smile. Wondering if her head ached this morning, he motioned for his brothers to be quiet. They looked startled, but nodded, toning down their voices and their laughter.

When Linda had eaten what she'd taken, he offered her more. He was pleased when she took another spoonful of eggs.

As she continued to eat, his stomach growled. He looked at his plate and realized he hadn't taken more than a bite or two while he watched her and Polly. Digging his fork into the mound of fried potatoes, he took a bite before saying, "Linda, I was thinking—"

"You thinking?" asked Micah with a muted chuckle. "That's no surprise."

"He always thinks everything to death," his twin added with a wink at Linda.

The comment annoyed Amos more than his brothers' interruption. He didn't want them flirting with her. *He* was the one who'd found her, and *he* had to make certain she was cared for until her memories returned. Startled by his reaction, because she wasn't a lost puppy anyone could claim, he kept his eyes on his plate as he continued, "I was thinking, Linda, you should come to the store today. We can retrace the steps you took yesterday to figure out what happened to you. I'm sure *Mamm* and Leah will be glad to entertain Polly."

Both women nodded before *Mamm* added, "Today is cookie-making day, and we could use help."

"Let me!" Polly bounced in her seat. "Can I help?"

"If Linda says it's okay." His *mamm* smiled at Mandy. "We won't make your favorite oatmeal raisin cookies until you get home from school."

"Linda?" The little girl looked at her as Mandy grinned in anticipation.

"*Ja.* You can stay and make cookies." She set her fork on her plate as the *kind* began to chatter with *Mamm* and Leah. To Amos, she added, "Are you sure she shouldn't come? She's sure to remember more than I do."

"I'm not sure how much value anything she remembers will be. It was growing dark by the time you reached the store."

Linda said nothing for a long minute, and he guessed she was considering his words. That was confirmed when she said, "You're right. Polly would try to help us, but expecting her to fill in the blanks is too much of a burden for a little girl. It'll be better for her to remain here."

Glad it was decided and trying not to notice how much he looked forward to spending the day with Linda, Amos began to eat with the same gusto as his brothers. He'd almost cleaned his plate when Mandy stood to leave the table.

After she'd dressed for the cold weather, his niece waved to everyone and went out the door, almost lost in her coat and scarf and hat. In her mittened hands, she carried a green lunch box.

"Where's she going?" Polly asked.

"To school," he and Linda said at the same time. He felt his face grow warm and wondered why he was flushing over such a silly thing. People frequently spoke at the same time. It didn't mean anything, did it?

The little girl ran to the window. "I want to go to school, too."

"When you're six," Linda replied.

"And I need you here to help me with cookies and helping me make up the extra beds in the *dawdi haus*," his *mamm* said.

"The *dawdi haus*?" Amos asked, astonished. "Are we having company for Christmas?"

"We already have company." She glanced at Linda. "Leah has enough to do taking care of you boys as well as her husband and Mandy. I thought it'd be nice for

Linda and Polly to stay with me." *Mamm* smiled as Polly waved to Mandy, who was trudging along the farm lane in the snow. "From the looks of them, I doubt either girl slept much during the night."

"I heard them giggling several times," Leah said as she brought the *kaffi* pot over to refill everyone's cups, including her own. "Separating them is a *gut* idea."

Amos couldn't argue with that and neither did Linda. As soon as he finished his breakfast, he stood. He asked Linda if she was ready to leave. She went to get her coat, her steps growing surer. When he realized he was staring after her, he averted his eyes. His gaze was caught by *Mamm*'s, and she arched her eyebrows before beginning to clear the table.

Her message was clear: *take care*. He'd told himself that over and over, aware of how little he knew about Linda. But he couldn't deny he was aware of the way her eyes crinkled when her lips tilted, of how her expression softened while she spoke with Polly, of how her lashes curled when she closed her eyes.

When Linda returned with her coat buttoned, Polly ran to her and grabbed her hand. "Come back. Please!" the little girl cried. "Don't leave me again."

"Did I leave you before?" Her eyes were bleak with dismay.

"*Ja*. Don't you remember?"

"I don't," she whispered. Squaring her shoulders, she said a bit more loudly, "Tell me about it."

"You told me to sit at the bus station while you asked someone something." The *kind* shuddered hard. "You went away for a long time. You came back. You didn't say a word till we got off the bus."

"Nothing?"

"No. You touched your head." The little girl's eyes filled with tears, and her lower lip quivered. "Poor you. You've got a bad boo-boo."

"I'm feeling much better, *liebling*. You don't need to worry about me leaving you. I won't. Not ever." She glanced over the little girl's head toward him.

He was astonished when he realized Linda wanted *him* to believe her. He bit back his instinctive reply that he couldn't imagine her abandoning the *kind* unless she had an important reason. But he didn't know her. And he didn't know what had happened to them.

Quietly he said, "There's a Philadelphia bus that passes through Paradise Springs during the late afternoon."

"How do you know that?" Hope brightened Linda's face. The hope she might rediscover what she'd lost.

"I sell bus tickets, and I keep the schedule posted at the store. The new one arrived last week. I noticed one bus route changed quite a bit, but the bus still stops in Paradise Springs."

She reached for the door. "Let's go. I want to see where else the bus might have stopped. Maybe something will jog my memory."

"I pray so." He wondered if he'd ever meant words more.

"This is a comfortable buggy," Linda said to make conversation as Amos drove toward his store. A plow must have come through during the night because snow was in foot-high banks on either side of the road.

"My oldest brother, Joshua, built it," he replied, holding the reins easily. "He's built or rebuilt almost every vehicle around Paradise Springs." He paused, then went on as if he didn't want the silence to return, "Pretty morning, ain't so?"

"Ja." She gazed across the sparkling countryside. The snow clinging to the tree branches plopped on the ground, making dark crevices in the brilliant white. She swallowed another yawn.

Her fingers tightened in her lap when she saw the sign for the Stoltzfus Family Shops in the distance. Amos drove to the far end of the empty parking lot. She eased the grip when her knuckles hurt, but she couldn't help being impatient. Was it possible? Could her past be jogged from her mind by looking at a bus schedule? It was a long shot because she wasn't sure where their journey had begun. She'd asked Polly to describe the bus station, but what the little girl could tell them didn't help Amos or his family guess which one it was.

Her gaze flicked toward the man sitting beside her. She hadn't known him a full day, but he seemed to be a trustworthy man from a *gut* family. Could she be sure of her impressions of anyone? Her mind was scrambled, and she was unsure where to turn.

Help me, God, to find the answers.

Amos stopped the buggy at the back of the building. Beyond the open space behind it was what looked like a smithy. He got out and started around the buggy. She didn't wait, stepping down on her own. She stumbled, almost falling to her knees, but a tight grip on the door's frame kept her on her feet.

Amos's jaw worked, but he said only, "Let me unlock the door." He walked to the small back porch. He left a trail of prints in his wake.

She looked at her feet. About six inches of snow had fallen during the night, and her sneakers were growing damp. She stepped onto the covered concrete porch. Shaking one foot, then the other, she watched packed snow fall off her soles. She needed boots if she planned to go anywhere, but how was she going to buy them? Other than the single penny she'd found in her dress pocket, she had no money.

Amos inserted a key and opened the door. He went in, and she heard him snap on the electric lights. A dull rumble of a propane furnace came to life as he toggled another switch.

"Where's the bus schedule?" she asked, unable to wait a minute more.

"This way." He walked past the first aisle to where a cash register was set on a counter. Beside it a pole held a bulletin board. In one corner, he'd tacked the bus schedule. She ran a finger along one column, then another.

"The bus that stops in Paradise Springs is this one," he said, reaching past her to touch the sixth column from the left.

She recoiled from his outstretched arm, cowering like an abused dog. She saw his shock. She was stunned, too. Why was she cringing away from a man who'd been nothing but kind to her and Polly? Did her senses remember something appalling that her mind had forgotten?

"The bus to Philadelphia," Amos said, his voice strained, "has stops to the west in Lancaster, York, Gettysburg and Chambersburg." He listed off more towns. "Any sound familiar?"

"I recognize most of those towns, but I don't remember visiting them. How far away from here does the bus stop?"

"Down by Route 30." He hesitated, then asked, "Why don't we walk toward the bridge and see if you remember anything?"

"Don't you need to open the store?"

"Nobody's here, so we have time to go to the bridge and back."

"I'd like to, but…" She glanced at her sneakers, then put her fingers to her head. Any motion, and she wasn't sure which one or when, could send a lightning flash of pain across her skull.

She didn't realize she was wobbling until Amos put his hand under her arm and urged her to stand still until she was steady. A moan rose from inside her. Not from the pain, but at how he was being nice when she'd acted, moments ago, as if she feared he was going to hurt her.

The darkness nibbling at the edge of her vision faded, and she raised her head and whispered, *"Danki."*

"Would you like to sit?"

Linda wanted to say *ja*, but even more she longed to remember her past. "Let's go to the bridge."

"Come with me." He motioned for her to follow him along the aisle.

Not sure why he'd turned away from the front door, she trailed after him.

He paused in front of a large wooden crate and pulled out a pair of black rubber boots. "These look to be your size."

She didn't take them. "I appreciate your offer, but I don't have—"

"Stop right there." His mouth grew taut. "I know you don't have any money. I'm not asking for any. Not now or later."

"But those boots must have cost you something."

"Look." He pointed to the box.

She saw it was filled with boots and mittens and hats and umbrellas and a few coats.

"Folks around here," he said, "leave clothes they can't use any longer in this box in case someone gets caught in a storm. You might as well use these boots for as long as you're here."

"I hope it won't be long until I can remember who I am and where we were going."

"I know. Sit down while you're putting them on, or you may tumble on your cute nose." He gestured toward a nearby bench as she felt heat climbing her cheeks at his unexpected compliment. "I put this here for my older customers to use if they needed a rest during their shopping. On warm fall days, after the harvest was in, it's a gathering place for farmers to discuss the prices they hoped to get for their crops and for boys to pick apart every detail of the World Series."

Sitting, she drew off her sneakers and reached for the boots. The world tilted, and she gripped the bench.

"Steady there," Amos said as he knelt and helped her slide her feet into the boots. He laced them closed, then looked at her. "Maybe this is too much today, Linda. We can do this another day."

"I don't want whoever's missing Polly and me to wait an extra day to learn where we are."

She saw his doubt that they'd discover anything today while her head was still unstable. She couldn't allow herself to believe her memories wouldn't return. She had to hold on to hope.

Standing, he put his hand under her arm and brought her to her feet. She steeled her knees so they wouldn't betray her. Without a word, he led her to the front door.

"Wait here while I lock the back door." He was gone before she could reply.

She looked out the door. Clouds were building to the west and the sunshine growing thin. Another storm? It was early in the year for such heavy snow.

Amos edged around her and opened the front door. She appreciated his taking care not to move his arm close to her. What *had* happened to her? She resisted touching the painful spot behind her ear. Had someone snuck up behind her and struck her? But why hadn't anyone seen that? Perhaps it had happened while she was alone, but why had she left Polly on her own in the first place? Nothing made sense.

She was beginning to wonder if it ever would.

Chapter Four

Linda stood by the concrete abutment at the far end of the bridge. Looking along the road curving toward the village of Paradise Springs, she paid no attention to the snowflakes drifting around her. The wind cut through her black wool coat, but it was not as icy as the fear inside her.

"I still don't remember anything before we reached the bridge. It's as if my life started the moment we crossed it." She put her mittens to her bonnet and frowned. "Why can't I remember anything?"

"Don't force it," Amos said. "That's what Dr. Montgomery said."

"*Ja.* I remember that, but why can't I remember anything else?" Raising her head, she blinked back tears. "I want to know what the doctor charged for coming to see me. I'll repay you as soon as I can."

"I know you will. Why don't you concentrate on getting better and leave other worries until later?"

"I know I should, but it's not easy to think of the future when I don't have any past to build upon."

He gave her the kind smile that eased the iciness around her frightened heart. "You've got this moment. That's all any of us have. This day, this moment the Lord has made for us. We can use it or waste it."

"That's a deep thought." She let her shoulders unstiffen as she gave in to the grin teasing her lips.

"I'm a deep thinking sort of man." He struck a pose worthy of a statue on a village green.

Her anxiety eased a bit as she laughed. She knew that was what he'd hoped she'd do because his dark brown eyes sparkled like sunshine. As more snow settled around them, muting the noise from cars out on the highway, she sent up a grateful prayer that Amos was the one who had found her and Polly. He and his family made her feel as if they were as invested in her recovering her memories as she was.

"I need to return to the store," he said as the snow continued to fall, harder with each passing second. "In case someone comes."

"All right." She didn't want to give in to failure, but standing in the storm wouldn't get her anything but a cold.

They walked toward the Stoltzfus Family Shops in silence. More than once she thought Amos was about to say something, but he didn't. She tried to think of something to say, but her head ached more with each step.

Another buggy was parked in front of Amos's store. It was a twin to the one she'd ridden in to the store, and

Linda recalled what Amos had said about his brother building or rebuilding many buggies in the area.

A tall man with a bushy gray beard stood by the store's front door. When he turned to watch them approach, she saw the man had wild, untamed gray eyebrows to match his beard. He smiled, and his face altered from forbidding to friendly.

Amos called a greeting, and the gray-bearded man stepped aside to let Amos unlock the door. "I never thought I'd see the day when you open late, Amos."

"Reuben," he replied, glancing over his shoulder at her, "this is a guest at our house. Her name is Linda." He motioned for her to join them. When she did, he added, "Reuben Lapp is our bishop."

"Hello," she said, trying to hide the many new questions scurrying through her battered mind. What was the name of the bishop in her home district? Did he smile as compassionately as Reuben did? Was she a baptized member, or had she not made that step to commit her life to her faith?

And if she'd been baptized, did that mean she was walking out with a young man she planned to marry? Plain women didn't wear wedding bands, so there was no way to know if a husband was trying to find her.

"Christmas season is a *gut* time for family and friends to visit, isn't it?" Reuben asked with a broadening smile.

She was saved from having to answer when Amos gave his bishop a quick explanation of what had happened last night. As the older man's expression grew serious, she wondered how many more people were going to be dismayed by her situation before her memories returned. She held her breath, hoping when Amos asked if Reuben had heard of anyone looking for a young woman and a little girl that his response would provide the answers she sought.

Her heart collapsed when the bishop shook his head. "I wish I had better news for you, Linda. I haven't heard of anybody missing a woman with the name Linda or a *kind* named Polly." Genuine compassion filled his eyes. "I'm sorry. I'll contact my fellow bishops and make other inquiries. You belong somewhere with people who must be missing you and the *kind*. We'll do what we can to reunite you with those who miss you." His smile returned. "The Amish grapevine is always efficient. News like this will spread quickly from family to family."

"Danki," she said as she followed Amos and the bishop into the store. She wasn't sure what she was going to do. Should she return to the Stoltzfus house and help Wanda and Leah with the day's chores?

Normally it'd be an easy walk, but between the snow and her own unsteadiness, she didn't trust herself to get there on her own. She stood by the door while Reuben completed his purchase. She nodded when the bishop, as he left the store, told her he'd immediately let her know any news he heard.

Amos came around the counter. "Are you all right? You look as gray as the sky."

"I'm as *gut* as I can be now."

"Reuben will do everything in his power—and in prayer—to find the truth for you."

"I know." She rubbed her hands together. "But I despise the thought of people frightened and worried because they don't know where we are."

"Think of how joyous your reunion will be."

She raised her gaze to meet his eyes which were darker with his strong emotions. "I wish I had your optimism."

"It's not optimism. It's faith God has a plan for you and your family, and His plan is a *gut* one."

"What *gut* can there be in losing my memory?"

He shrugged. "You're asking the wrong guy. You need to ask God."

"I have been asking. Over and over."

"He'll answer. He always does." He gave her a grin. "Just not always on our schedule."

She returned his smile, feeling the weight on her shoulders ease. "*Danki* for the reminder." Her laugh surprised her as much as him when she added, "I need reminders about everything."

He shook his head. "No, you haven't needed a reminder about loving Polly. Though the situation looks bleak, think how much worse it would have been if you didn't recall anything about her."

"You *are* an optimist."

"Guess I'm guilty as charged. Or maybe it's this time of year. It's hard to be grim when we're surrounded by happiness. So many weddings and the Christmas holidays and the snow that's pretty when it blankets the ground and hushes the world." Looking past her toward the empty parking lot, he asked, "Would you consider coming to the store tomorrow?"

"Why?"

"Tomorrow is Saturday, and the store is always busy. Maybe one of my customers will recognize you." He laughed. "Maybe I should set up one of those games like *Englisch* shopkeepers do, but instead of guessing how many gumballs are in the jar, people can guess what your last name is." He shook his head with another chuckle. "Not that it'd be much of a challenge with so many Stoltzfuses, Millers, Yoders and Beilers around here."

She laughed along with him, ignoring the unending questions while she did. No matter what happened after she learned the truth of who she was, one thing wouldn't change. She'd forever be grateful to Amos Stoltzfus for lifting her out of her fears with the lilt of laughter.

The church Sunday service was being held about a mile away at the Chupp family's farm. Linda doubted Amos and his family would have hitched up their buggy horses except for the fact that she found it difficult to walk any distance.

Yesterday, her hopes had been dashed. Nobody who came into the store had recognized her, though Amos had asked every customer, plain and *Englisch*, if they did. Some had glanced at her and shrugged, but many had considered the question before they answered. Each time the answer was the same: they'd never seen her before. That meant she couldn't have been coming to Paradise Springs. Why had she and Polly gotten off the bus here?

"You stood and said it was time to go," Polly had told her when they went to bed in the cozy upstairs room in the *dawdi haus* last night. While she'd been at the store, Amos's brothers had moved two twin beds into the small space with its slanting ceilings and dormer window. "You didn't say anything else."

Maybe the bus tickets would point to where they were bound, but searching her pockets had revealed nothing. She asked Polly to check her own pockets. Nothing. If they'd had printed tickets, they'd been lost somewhere. Maybe she'd left them on the bus. Maybe they had slipped from her fingers on the walk to Amos's store. Finding them beneath the snow would be next to impossible.

And Linda was too exhausted for such a task. Nightmares had kept Polly awake through the night. What the little girl dreamed seemed to vanish as soon as Polly woke, crying in fright, but she knew someone bad was chasing them. Was it a memory, or was the little girl prone to night terrors? Yet another question with no answer.

When they reached the farm where the service would take place, Polly stayed close to Linda. The little girl's hand held on so tightly Linda's fingers began to cramp. She readjusted Polly's grip, but didn't let go of her hand.

"There are lots of *kinder* here," she said to reassure the little girl.

"Do you think they'll like me and play with me?"

"*Ja*, but not until after the worship service."

Polly gave her a disgusted glance. "I know, Linda. I'm not a *boppli*."

A lighthearted, resonating laugh startled Linda. She turned, knowing who stood behind them. Why hadn't

Amos joined his brothers and the other men by the front porch where they were gathering before they were called inside for the worship service?

Her head spun, and she knew she'd moved too quickly. Her heart had propelled her around before her mind could warn her to be careful. She raised her eyes to meet his gaze, and he put his broad fingers on her arm. Warmth swirled through her, but oddly it didn't blur everything in front of her. Instead, she felt more grounded than she had since she woke on the sofa in his family's front room.

"If you feel too lousy to stay," he said in a whisper, "I can take you home at any time." He spoke quietly, she realized, because he worried that her headache had returned with a vengeance.

What a *gut* man he was! It would be so easy to listen to her heart that was pleading for her to risk it and tell him how much his kindness meant to her. She couldn't. Not when she had no idea if she was betrothed or married. "I'll be fine."

"I'm sure you will." His smile warmed her in spite of the icy wind. "You're a determined woman, and I suspect you can do whatever you put your mind to."

"How can you say that? You don't know me." She swallowed her gasp when he flinched as if she'd struck him. What had she said that upset him so much? Unsure, she kept going, hoping that her next words would bring back his smile. "*I* don't know me." She tried a laugh, but it was feeble and sounded fake even to her own ears.

When his name was called, Amos excused himself and went to join the men. She watched his easy lope

through the snow. To look at him, nobody would guess
he had anything on his mind other than what he wanted
to discuss with his friends.

When the women entered the house, Linda wasn't
surprised Polly clung to her hand and to Wanda's.
Amos's *mamm* treated Polly as if she were one of her
own *kins-kinder.* Her other grandchildren were giggling
together behind them.

Linda sat with the rest of the *maedels* on a bench
behind the married women. The *kinder* were scattered among the adults, some sitting with the women
and a few of the boys with the men. Pushing aside any
thoughts but of the moment, she joined in with the first
hymn. She savored the slow pace of the music. Her heart
drew in strength from the community of faith. When
the congregation began the next song, *"Das Loblied,"*
which was always sung as the second hymn, she let the
opening words of the second verse sink into her:

Oh may thy servant be endowed
With wisdom from on high

She longed for wisdom to open the place where her
memories were sealed away. Smiling at Polly, she raised
her eyes and saw Amos watching her from across the
room. He was a fine-looking man, standing a full head
taller than the men on either side of him. When he
looked away, his mouth hardening for a moment, she
was startled. Why would he be upset she was staring at
him when *he* had been studying her openly?

Linda sat as a minister moved to the center of the

room to begin his sermon. He had the same height the Stoltzfus brothers possessed and resembled Amos, though his jaw was partially hidden beneath an uneven beard. Her guess was confirmed when Wanda whispered, "That's my third son, Isaiah."

Unsure if she'd met Isaiah the night she woke in the Stoltzfuses' living room and wondering which woman sitting among the married women was his wife, she listened as he began the longer sermon. She became enmeshed in the words as he spoke from the heart with an eloquence she wasn't surprised to hear from Amos's older brother.

Isaiah must be like Amos in more than the shape of his face. They both were deep thinkers. That was confirmed as he spoke on the subject of forgiveness.

"Even the most heinous act," Isaiah said with quiet dignity, "needs to be forgiven. We all know that, but we often forget that we must let that transgression be forgotten, as well."

She froze on the bench. Was she trying to forget something too horrible to remember? A shiver sliced down her spine.

What if what happened to her and Polly had been so appalling her mind had let go of everything in order to forget it?

Amos shifted on the church bench. His twin brothers glanced at him, and he halted. The last time he'd been antsy during church services was when he was not much older than Polly.

But it wasn't easy to sit still when, in the middle of

his brother's sermon, he saw color wash from Linda's face. Was she in pain? She put her arm around Polly and slanted the *kind* against her. Her gaze flicked in his direction, sweeping away. Not before he saw the raw emotion in her eyes. Was it fear?

Maybe she'd remembered something. No, he didn't want to think of her recovered memories being so frightening, but he should be thankful she'd recalled something. She could return to her life…and he could stop thinking about her. Wouldn't that be for the best? He'd made an idiot of himself over one lovely woman, and Linda's recovery would keep him from doing so again. He'd noticed the glances his *mamm* had aimed at him while he was laughing with Linda. *Mamm* had worn a similar smile when his brothers grew serious about the women who became their wives.

But he wasn't walking out with Linda. He was trying to help her find the truth by regaining her memories. For all he knew, she was another man's wife. That thought hit him in the gut like an enraged billy goat. He didn't like thinking of her belonging with someone else.

He had to keep reminding himself how important it was to be certain. More and more with each passing day because Linda was becoming a part of his life. When he wasn't with her, thoughts of her filled his head. Unlike her, he couldn't forget anything: her kindness to Polly, her willingness to help at the store, the easy way she made him smile and laugh as he hadn't in far too long.

Amos scrambled to his feet when he realized others were standing. He'd lost track of the service, and Reuben was ending it with *"Da Herr sei mit du."*

He replied with the rest of the congregation, "And the Lord be with you, too."

His plan to ask Linda what was amiss went awry. He had to help rearrange some of the benches into tables for the communal meal, then his brothers insisted he join them to eat. Linda wasn't one of the women bringing the food from the kitchen. Wolfing down his sandwich and excusing himself, he went to find her.

Everywhere he looked she'd been moments ago. How could it be difficult to find her in the farmhouse? His search was interrupted by friends who wanted to draw him into conversations. He didn't want to be rude, but he needed to know why Linda's face had become ashen. Even after the women and *kinder* had finished their meals, he hadn't found her. Had she eaten in the kitchen? He'd check there again.

As he passed a living room window, he saw Linda standing in the front yard. He yanked his coat off the pile on the sofa. Grabbing a scarf and a hat and gloves, he didn't pay any attention if they were his. He didn't want to waste time looking for his own, because if he took his eyes off her, she might vanish.

The chilly breeze was gone, and the sunshine was melting snow from the roof and nearby trees. A clump of half-frozen snow found its way down his collar. When he yelped, Linda looked toward him. When he exaggerated shaking his coat to let the frigid remnants fall behind him, she gave him the smile he'd hoped for.

He ignored the warning crashing through his head. He shouldn't be so eager for her smiles. He was getting in too deep with a woman who might not be free to flirt with him. "Why are you out in the cold?"

"Keeping an eye on Polly." She pointed at where the *kinder* slid on a snowy hill in the pasture beyond the barn. "I don't know if she's gone sledding before."

"Why didn't you join her?"

Her smile faded. "You know why. I can't risk banging my head. Remember what the *doktorfraa* said? I could do greater damage, and I might never get my memories back."

He hadn't forgotten, but he doubted a tumble off a sled into the soft snow would do her any damage. Yet he understood her hesitation. She'd lost everything but Polly when she'd been hurt before. She couldn't risk injuring herself worse.

"Wait here," he said.

"But—"

"I wouldn't let you hurt yourself. Don't you know that?"

She paused for so long he wondered if she wanted to avoid an answer; then she said, "*Ja*, I trust you."

Her soft reply sent skyrockets soaring through him. Somehow managing a steady voice to tell her again to wait where she was, he trotted toward the barn before he had to say anything else. He wasn't sure he could speak more without stumbling over his words like a teenager asking a girl to walk out with him. Her confidence in him meant more than she could guess because he'd had trouble trusting himself after Arlene made such a public fool of him. How could he have guessed she'd loudly list what she considered his shortcomings in the midst of a taffy pull and in front of their friends? His attempts to hush her and to take the argument outside away from everyone else only made her shriller. He knew he wasn't perfect. No one was, but he'd been shocked by her anger and indiscretion their last evening as a couple. Only later did he discover that she had been walking out with other men while letting him believe he was the special one for her. He knew he was letting bruised pride get in the way, but his efforts to move past it had failed.

Until the simple words *I trust you* showed him the way.

But he needed more. He needed the assurance he knew Linda. Really knew her, instead of being beguiled by her lovely face and gentle heart.

He shouldn't be thinking about that. He was simply taking her and Polly sledding. Grabbing what he wanted from a shelf inside the door, he jogged to where Linda waited.

He smiled as he handed her a black bicycle helmet. When she looked at it, puzzled, he said, "The *kinder* wear these when they ride their scooters. Steven McMurray, the local police chief, has been urging parents to get them for their kids if they plan to ride along the roads. With the dips and rises on these twisting roads, a *kind* could come over the top of a hill and not be able to stop in time to make a corner." He chuckled. "I suspect Dr. Montgomery talked Chief McMurray into the whole idea, but it's a *gut* one."

She examined it from every angle. "Do you think it'll keep me safe?"

"I think it will protect your head. I can't claim it'll do anything else." He grinned. "But we'll stick to the gentler hills, and let the teenagers take the challenging slopes."

"How do I put it on?" She turned it around and around. "Both ends look pretty much the same, and I'm not sure which is the front and which is the back."

"Let me." He took the helmet from her. Turning it so the front faced him, he stepped closer. "Let me know if anything I do hurts you."

"I doubt that's possible," she murmured. She trusted him. He wished trust was as easy for him.

He shook the past from his head, knowing he shouldn't complain about troublesome memories. At least he had his memories. No matter how bad they might be, losing them as she had would be terrible. He settled the helmet over her bonnet. Taking the straps, he hooked them beneath her chin without crushing her head covering.

"Is that comfortable?" he asked.

"A little tight."

He reached to loosen the straps, but as soon as his fingers brushed her cheek, they refused to move. They lingered against her soft, cool skin. She kept her eyes lowered, and he wondered if she felt the same rush of delight he did. If so, she was acting smarter than he was.

He led the way through the pasture gate and toward the hill. More than once, he considered taking her hand to help her through the snow, but didn't. If he enfolded her fingers in his, he wasn't sure he'd be able to let them go.

Polly ran up to them, jabbering about the rides she'd taken down the hill. Snow was ingrained in her wool coat, and her cheeks were a brilliant red. Her eyes glittered as brightly as the snow as she urged them to join her.

Amos borrowed a sled and positioned it at the top of the hill. It was long enough for Linda to sit in front of him with her arms around Polly. His heart danced in his chest like a runaway horse when he reached forward to grasp the ropes connected to the front. He'd have liked to slip his arm around Linda and draw her closer, but he needed to steer. There were trees flanking the hill. If the sled started heading for one side or the other, he needed to be able to pull it into the center of the hill. He couldn't let there be the slightest chance Linda was injured.

Polly shrieked with excitement as he pushed off before putting his feet against the steering bar at the front. His breath burst from him as Linda pressed back while the sled picked up speed. When they hit a bump and she rocked to one side, he clamped his arm around her waist as she did the same to the *kind*.

His eyes widened. They were going too fast. They weren't going to stop before the fence. He jammed his left boot against the bar, and the sled skidded to the side. Leaning, he shouted a warning as they toppled into the snow, skidding along with the empty sled.

As soon as he stopped, Amos clambered to his knees and looked for Linda and Polly. He saw them sprawled in the snow.

"Are you okay?" he called.

His answer was a handful of snow thrust into his face. As he sputtered, he heard Linda laughing along with Polly. Not a strained laugh or a weak one. Her laughter was genuine and burst out of her, unrestrained.

"What did you do that for?" he asked, wiping away flakes.

She laughed. "You dumped us in the snow."

"To keep us from hitting the fence."

"I got snow in my face, so it's fair you did, too."

"Fair? I'm not sure what's fair about it." He pointed at the fence. "I saved you from hitting that."

"Maybe. Maybe not." She glanced at Polly who giggled. "Want to ride again?"

The little girl cheered, jumped up and ran to get the sled. As Linda stood, brushing herself off, her eyes were as bright as the *kind*'s. She helped Polly pull the sled up the hill.

Looking over her shoulder, Linda asked, "Coming?"

She didn't wait for his answer as he stood to follow.

Ja, he'd help them go fast down the hill. But he knew one thing. With Linda, he needed to take it slow. This time if he made a mistake, he could hurt her—and Polly—as much as he hurt himself.

Chapter Five

As soon as the school Christmas program on the first day of winter was over, Polly ran to hug Mandy and her cousin Debbie at the front of the schoolroom. Polly adored the two girls and followed them everywhere after school, and the two older girls always welcomed her.

Linda smiled as the girls showed Polly the display the scholars had made and hung on the blackboard. It was covered with pictures of the Nativity drawn on every possible shade of construction paper. *Joy to the World* was spelled in block letters on red and green sheets above the windows on one side of the room.

The school felt familiar. Desks were lined up five across for six rows. They faced the teacher's desk set by the blackboard. Everything looked exactly as she'd expected it to.

Linda was sure she must have attended a school like this, but was she also a teacher as Amos's younger sister Esther had been before her recent wedding? She tried to imagine herself teaching a class filled with *kinder* from six to fourteen years old. Glancing at the books stacked on the bookcase beneath one window, she knew their titles by the colors of the spines. Was it because she'd studied with similar books, or had she taught with them? If she was a teacher, that meant she wasn't married.

Her gaze went, before she could halt it, toward where Amos was talking with his *mamm*. He glanced at Linda and a slow, warm smile curved along his lips. The too-familiar quiver in her middle warned her to look away.

She couldn't. The buzz of conversations filling the room faded as he walked toward her. Would he brush his fingers against her cheek as he had on Sunday before they went sledding with Polly? Even four days later, her skin heated in anticipation of his gentle touch, though she knew he wouldn't be brash when his family and neighbors stood nearby.

"You look unsettled," he said quietly, though nobody was paying any attention as parents congratulated the scholars for remembering the lines they'd worked hard to memorize.

Linda sighed. "I am." She explained how she recognized the textbooks. "Why can I remember the name of the third grade reader, but I don't know my own last name?"

"Why are you unhappy you've recovered another memory? It may not be the one you hope for, but it's a memory, and it's yours."

"You're right. It's my memory. It's mine." She spoke

those words like a prayer, then sent up a true prayer of gratitude to God for what she was able to recall.

And for Amos.

He was a steady rock in the storms swirling around her.

"I don't know if I could be as patient as you are," he said, leaning one hand on a nearby chair.

"What gave you the idea I'm patient?"

"You aren't stomping around displaying your frustration over the whole situation."

"I would if it'd help." She smiled at him. "Do you think it would?"

"If I say *ja*, will you stamp around?"

She appreciated his teasing that drew her out of her doldrums. If not for Amos, it'd be far too easy to give in to the grief tugging at her whenever she let her guard down.

Polly ran to them. "Mandy says she's going to teach me the songs they sang today, even the ones with *Englisch* words!"

"Isn't that *wunderbaar*?" Linda asked.

"Ja." The little girl dimpled. "I'm glad we're here. I miss *Grossmammi* and *Grossdawdi*, but Mandy is my bestest friend!"

Linda kept her smile in place, but it wasn't easy. She couldn't miss Polly's grandparents—whoever they might be—because she remembered nothing about them.

"And you're her friend," Amos said. "Hers and Debbie's."

"Debbie says I'm *gut* to practice on. Her little sister is a *boppli*."

"That she is." He stood straighter. "But she's growing fast."

Polly turned to her. "Linda, let's get a *boppli*, too."

Sure every ear in the room had heard Polly's question, Linda hoped her face was not as red as it felt. "A *boppli* needs a *mamm* and a *daed*."

"I know that." The little girl regarded her with an expression that suggested Linda was the silly one. She looked at Amos. "You can be the *daed*."

Every word Linda had ever known fled from her mind, but Amos laughed and bent to look at the *kind*. "You've got everything planned, don't you?"

"Ja!"

"Can you keep a secret?" he asked in a conspiratorial tone.

Polly nodded eagerly.

"You won't tell anyone?"

"No."

"Not even Linda?"

The little girl hesitated, torn between needing to know what he had to say and knowing she'd want to share it with Linda.

Amos chuckled. "All right. You can tell Linda, but nobody else. Okay?"

She nodded and grinned. "What is it?"

Putting his hand next to his mouth, he bent to whisper in the little girl's ear. Linda couldn't hear what he said, but Polly's smile returned, growing wider with every passing second. Linda wondered what he was saying to the *kind* about her expectations.

Her naive expectations, Linda knew. But why was

her own mind filled with images of her and Amos standing together and watching Polly participate in a Christmas program? Smaller *kinder*, their *kinder*, would be gathered around them, as eager as Polly was now.

Had she lost her mind as well as her memories? Mistaking Amos's kindness for anything else would be the worst thing she could do.

Amos drew back as Polly crowed, "Hooray! We're going to have *snitz* pie tonight!" She put a finger to her lips. "Don't tell anyone. It's a secret."

"I won't," Linda said, astonished how easily Amos had turned the little girl's mind to other matters. She smiled over Polly's head and mouthed, *"Danki."*

He winked in response, and the motion sent another rush of warmth cascading through her. He cared as much about the little girl as she did.

She and Polly had spent a week at the Stoltzfus farm, and the odd situation of not knowing who she was and where she'd come from almost seemed normal. Depending on Amos to cheer her up when she felt blue was becoming a habit, too. She wished she could be sure if it were a *gut* one or not.

When Linda went with Polly to see Mandy's desk, Amos remained where he was. He couldn't tag after Linda like a puppy. That would cause more talk about the mysterious woman who'd appeared during a snowstorm. Nobody was unkind. Simply curious, and he couldn't fault them, because he wanted to know the truth about her, as well.

He pulled his gaze from where she stood by a desk

with Mandy and Polly. *Mamm* was talking with Neva Fry, the new teacher. She'd done a *gut* job stepping in when she took over the responsibilities of the school and its scholars after his younger sister Esther married Nathaniel Zook two weeks ago. The newlyweds and the young boy who lived with them were visiting Nathaniel's family in Indiana for the holidays. Otherwise, Esther wouldn't have missed seeing the program.

It had been a splendid one. He listened to Polly join in each time a song was sung in *Deitsch*. The *kind* wouldn't learn to speak *Englisch* until she went to school, so when the carols were in *Englisch*, Linda whispered a translation into her ear. Though Linda had lost much, she hadn't forgotten her love for the *kind*.

He could admit to himself he was glad the *kind* had confirmed Linda wasn't her *mamm*. That was the one fact he was sure of. Watching Linda from the corner of his eye, he wondered—as he had many times before— why she'd been traveling with only a little girl. Surely if she had a husband, he would have come with them.

Amos knew he shouldn't let her become more a part of his life. He'd made a mistake over another woman, and he'd been certain he knew Arlene well. He couldn't say he knew Linda. She hid much of herself, more than what her lost memories could account for. Maybe she didn't want to make too many connections in Paradise Springs until she discovered where she belonged.

"Amos?" *Mamm*'s tone suggested she'd called to him more than once.

"Sorry. I was…thinking."

"I can see." She gave him an indulgent smile.

"Could you bring Linda and Polly home in your buggy? Leah's is full."

"I hope you aren't trying to matchmake, *Mamm*."

"I leave that to the professional matchmakers."

He arched a brow, and she chuckled. "*Ja*, Linda and Polly can ride in my buggy."

"*Danki*, Amos. We'll see you there. Don't be late, or your brothers will devour your share of the *snitz* pie."

Laughing, he said, "I won't be late. Nobody wants to miss your famous *snitz* pie, *Mamm*."

"Hardly famous," she chided, but he could tell she was pleased at his compliment for her dried apple pie.

His *mamm* walked away to speak with a neighbor, and he headed toward Mandy's desk to let Linda know of the change in plans.

As he approached, he heard Polly saying, "I liked when you used to read stories to me, Linda."

"You did?"

"I like stories before I go to bed. You used to read to me every night. Until…" The light in the little girl's eyes became cloudy with distress.

Linda's face flushed, then went gray, but her voice gave no sign of her thoughts as she said, "I think we should have a story before bed tonight and every night. What do you think?"

"*Ja!*" She pressed her cheek against Linda and whispered, "*Ich liebe dich,* Linda."

"I love you, too."

Something in Amos's chest loosened when he watched the two embrace. Was it his tight hold on his heart? He'd guarded it since Arlene had tossed it aside like last week's newspaper. Never had he imagined a pint-size *kind* would break the chokehold he'd kept in place for five years. No, not Polly, but Linda who couldn't hide her love for the little girl. He wondered what it'd be like to have her love him.

He stepped aside as several of the scholars' parents and grandparents paused to ask Linda how she was feeling. Her smile appeared to be genuine, but he noticed how her hands curled into fists before she concealed them behind her back. Their well-intentioned words were a reminder of how much she had lost.

If Linda's smile grew any more brittle, it was going to crack off her face. Amos wondered how much longer her composure could hold together. She looked exhausted, and he reminded himself it'd been only a little over a week since he'd found her, lost and in pain, in the parking lot.

He waited for a break in the conversation. "We need to leave," he said in his most casual tone when that pause came. "I've got to make a stop before we head home."

Linda nodded, but he could sense her relief as she said goodbye to the crowd. Taking Polly by the hand, she squatted to help the *kind* button her coat. She didn't notice the looks exchanged over her head, but he did.

He was glad she hadn't, because she would have been bothered by the sympathetic expressions. He bit back words he must not speak. The concern was meant kindly, but it made Linda uncomfortable. She hadn't given any quarter to the pain or her lost memories, and she didn't want to be seen as an object of pity.

Dusk was changing to dark on the shortest day of the year when Amos led the way to his buggy. Linda hadn't acted as if riding home with him was anything out of the ordinary. Because she didn't see him as someone she'd walk out with?

Polly chattered about what she'd seen, and Amos was grateful because he wasn't sure what to say to Linda when his thoughts were completely out of his control.

He broke the silence when they turned on the road leading through the middle of Paradise Springs. "I need to stop at the store, but I can take you to the farm first."

"I thought you were making an excuse at the school."

He shook his head as he glanced at the *Englisch* houses. Christmas lights twinkled on the eaves of many of them. "I need to stop at the store because of a late delivery, but like I said, I can take you home first."

"Nonsense. The store is on our way. Patch won't be happy to see his comfortable stable and then have to go out."

"How about me? You have sympathy for my horse, but none for me?"

"I assume if you don't want to go back out, you won't." She smiled, and he realized she was teasing him.

That pleased him. She was serious too often, and, when she jested with his family, he saw shadows of uncertainty and despair in her eyes. It was a constant reminder how her family must be anxious about where she and Polly were.

He kept the jesting going until he'd unlocked the front door and turned on the store's lights. Hearing a rumble on the road, he went to the window. The delivery truck from the warehouse that supplied his store was pulling into the parking lot.

"This won't take long," he said as he unwound his scarf and tossed it and his coat on the checkout counter. "I need to do a quick inventory to make sure everything matches the invoice."

"Can I help?" Linda asked.

He was about to tell her he could handle it himself as he always did, but he smiled. "Sure. It'll go more quickly with two of us working. I'm sure the driver will be glad, too."

While Polly raced up one aisle and down the other, pausing to look at any container that caught her eye, Linda followed him into the storage room. He opened the door, and the back-up beeps of the large truck became shrill. Taking his handcart from a dim corner, he pushed it onto the covered rear porch.

"Hello, Mac," he said to the truck driver. "Working late tonight?"

The older man, whose belly strained against his coat, grimaced. "These deliveries have to be made before Christmas, or the boss will get upset." He rolled his eyes. "And it's never a good idea to get the boss upset."

Amos took the invoices before the driver opened the truck and let down a ramp. Handing the pages to Linda, Amos asked her to put a check next to the line for each box as it came into the store.

"Do you have a highlighter?" she asked. "It'd be easier to see any missing items with one."

"That's a *gut* idea for next time."

She nodded and bent over the list as he helped unload

the boxes and the bags of flour and sugar. He realized it was odd how he'd never invited Arlene to be part of his life at the store. Or maybe not odd because she'd never shown any interest. Most of their conversations had revolved around the intriguing gossip she adored.

On the other hand, it was too easy to imagine Linda working by his side again. He looked at where she made a neat check next to each item as he called it off. With her head bowed over the pages, a single strand of her white-blond hair fluttered against her cheek on the cold air blowing into the room. It took every bit of his strength not to push it behind her ear.

When everything was unloaded, Mac bid them a merry Christmas and shut the truck. Amos closed the door and locked it. As he turned, his gaze was caught by Linda's. Her face was blank, but many emotions swirled through her eyes. He felt dizzy. Or was the light-headedness because they stood close together in the otherwise—save for a four-year-old *kind*—deserted store?

Look away! The warning blared in his head, but he couldn't obey it. He took one step, then another toward her, closing the distance between them. He half expected her to turn and walk away. She remained where she was, her fingers clutching the invoice papers.

"Everything checked out," she said in an unsteady whisper. The strand of hair now curved along her face as he wished his fingers were.

"*Danki* for your help." He edged nearer.

"I'm glad to help. You and your family have done so much for Polly and me."

His hand rose of its own volition toward that enticing tress. Her name burst from him in a breathy whisper as he touched her cheek.

"Are you here, Amos?" came a deeper voice from the front of the store. "Is Linda here, too?"

Amos jerked his hand back as if he'd grabbed a lightning bolt. He avoided looking at Linda as he went to where his bishop stood by the front door. Reuben was listening as Polly tried to tell him every detail of the school program.

"Reuben, is there something in particular you're looking for?" Amos asked when the little girl was finished.

The bishop nodded. "I'm assuming Linda is here if Polly is."

"Ja." Dozens of questions pounded his lips, but he didn't let a single one escape.

When the bishop looked past him, Amos peered over his shoulder at where Linda stood in the door to the back room. She walked to Amos and handed him the invoices as if she helped at the store every day.

"Guten owed, Reuben," she said.

"Good evening to you, too." He drew in a deep breath and let it flow out in an extended sigh. "I hope I'm not going to ruin it by what I have to tell you."

"The truth may be harsh, but it's better when it's not half-hidden in niceties."

Reuben nodded, clearly pleased with her answer. Amos tried to ignore the pulse of pride bursting inside him. She was *wunderbaar,* a gutsy woman unwilling to buckle under the challenges she faced.

"Then," said the bishop, "I'll get right to the point and say the news isn't *gut*. I've contacted bishops between here and Lancaster. Each of them has asked members of their districts, and nobody reports knowing you and Polly."

She sank to the bench by the door and clasped her hands in her lap. "Oh..."

Amos looked at Reuben, and the bishop motioned for him to remain quiet. He understood needing to let Linda respond before he jumped in; yet, it was almost impossible not to offer her comfort. Not just words, but drawing her into his arms and holding her until he could find the right thing to say.

She raised her head, and he knew her courage had not wavered. Her eyes were bright with tears, but none streaked her face. When she spoke, her voice was more unwavering than his would have been if their situations were reversed.

"*Danki* for your efforts to help find Polly's and my family." She closed her eyes and sighed. "Or maybe I should say families." Looking at him and Reuben, she added, "Either way, I appreciate your help."

"Don't give up," his bishop said in his kindest tone. "More people are being contacted. This search is spreading like ripples in a pond. We've assumed you took the bus from Lancaster, but there are connections at that station to many places. We won't give up until we know the truth, either by you regaining your memories or someone coming forward."

When she repeated her gratitude as Polly climbed

into her lap and put her arms around Linda's neck, she hugged the *kind*.

Amos walked Reuben onto the porch and added his own thanks.

"It's difficult to be away from those we love during the Christmas season," Reuben said, "but at least we have our memories to comfort us. Linda has nothing."

"She has Polly, and she has her faith this will be set to rights. Somehow."

"And she has you, Amos."

"My whole family has pitched in."

"*Ja*, but you've set yourself up as her earthly protector." Reuben put a workworn hand on Amos's shoulder. "Be careful, son. Once her memories return, everything may be different."

"I think of that constantly."

Bidding Amos a good night, the bishop vanished into the night. The creak of springs and leather told Amos when Reuben had climbed into his buggy.

Amos went inside and paused to select a bag of lollipops. Opening it, he offered it to Polly. "You were such a *gut* girl at the program. Pick two or three to take home with you."

"And for Mandy?"

Touched by her generosity, he smiled. "Take two or three for her, too."

"And Debbie?"

"Maybe it'd be simpler if you take the whole bag. Go and get your coat, because we don't want my brothers to finish off the *snitz* pie before we get there. Lollipops are *gut*, but not as *gut* as *Mamm*'s pie."

With an excited shout, Polly ran to the far end of the store where she'd left her coat and mittens.

As soon as the *kind* was out of earshot, Amos asked, *"Bischt allrecht?"*

"*Ja*, I'm all right." Linda stood and smoothed her apron over her dress. "Nothing's changed, has it?"

He nodded, knowing it was true. No matter how much he wanted everything to change, for her to regain her memories and for him to be certain there was no other man in her heart, nothing had. He was beginning to wonder if it ever would and what they—what *he* would do if her memories never returned.

Chapter Six

The bedroom Linda shared with Polly in the *dawdi haus* had a view of the snow-covered pastures. Paw prints crisscrossed the field, showing where rabbits and a fox had traveled. Tinier marks pinpointed the landing spots of birds. Evergreens bent toward the ground with their burdens of snow, but bare branches were a lacy pattern against the bright blue sky.

It was a lovely, albeit chilly morning three days before Christmas, and, as she sat on her bed and stared out the window, Linda faced a troubling dilemma. Christmas was coming, and she had no gifts for the Stoltzfus family. She wanted to buy them gifts, but how could she? She didn't have any money.

"Was iss letz?" Polly asked, climbing onto the bed beside her.

"What makes you think something is wrong?" she asked the little girl.

"You look like a cloud on a stormy day."

In spite of her low spirits, Linda smiled. "Did you make that up yourself?"

Polly shook her head. "No. I heard *Mamm* say it a lot."

"What else did she say?" she asked. Polly hadn't said much about her parents, and the key to unlocking Linda's memories might be in one of Polly's recollections.

The little girl shrugged. "Lots of things."

"Tell me." She put her arm around Polly's small shoulders.

Polly screwed up her face in concentration. "She told me *gut* deeds have echoes, but I've never heard any."

"It means if you do something nice for someone, that person may be happy and do something *gut* for someone else."

"Like when I ask Mandy for some milk and we have cookies together?"

"*Ja*. Like that." She was delighted by Polly's perspective which always seemed to have something to do with Mandy and cookies. "Did Mandy tell you we'll be making sweets tomorrow for the cookie exchange on Christmas Eve?"

"Yummy." She grew serious as she asked, "Linda, can we get Mandy something special for Christmas?"

"You could make her—"

"No! I want to get her what she wants. A book about a little house and the woods."

Little House in the Big Woods, Linda translated. She'd heard Mandy mention the book more than once in the past few days.

"I'm sorry, Polly, I don't have any money to buy her a book."

"I've got money."

Linda stared at the *kind*. "You do?"

"*Ja*. Lots of it. Wait here." She jumped down from the bed and ran to pull her coat from a peg by the door. What was the *kind* doing?

Rooting around in one pocket and then the other, Polly drew out a cloth bag. She put her coat on a nearby chair before returning to Linda. "See?"

Linda took the bag, expecting to feel a few coins in it. Her eyes widened when she heard the crackle of paper. She undid the drawstring and peered in. She gasped. The bag was filled with money. Pulling it out, she counted in astonishment.

Why would anyone give a *kind* more than fifty dollars?

She didn't realize she'd asked the question aloud until Polly said, "You gave it to me, Linda. You asked me to take *gut* care of it."

She tried to remember doing what Polly had described. Nothing. The same gray cloud of nothingness filled her mind, standing between the woman she was now and the person she'd been before…before whatever had happened at the bus station.

Knowing that trying to recover a memory seemed to make it flee from her, she looked at the money in her hand. Instead of wondering why she'd given money to a young *kind*, she should be grateful she had it. She could buy gifts for Mandy and the rest of the Stoltzfus family.

"Put on your coat, Polly. We're going shopping."

"Yippee!" She ran to obey.

Linda found a sheet of paper and wrote a quick note to let Wanda know where they were going and why. She finished it with *We'll be back in a few hours.* Setting it on the table in the *dawdi haus*'s tiny living room, she put on her boots and, grabbing her own coat, flung it on as she walked to the door dividing the living room from the main house.

"Leah, can I use your buggy this morning?" she called into the kitchen.

"Of course. If you need help hitching the horse up, ask Ezra. He's in the barn." Her eyes crinkled in a smile. "He's working on a new type of cheese today, so I'm sure he'll be there to unhitch the horse when you get back. Nobody's going to budge him out of the cheese room today."

"Danki." Holding her hand out to Polly, she closed the connecting door. She was as excited as the little girl was to select gifts to thank the Stoltzfus family for their warm hospitality. She had ideas about what to get each one…except Amos.

How was she going to find him a gift that would express what he meant to her when she wasn't sure herself? No, that wasn't the truth. She *knew* she was falling in love with him, whether she should or not.

How long before he paced a path right through the floor? How many more looks could *Mamm* aim at him, each a silent reprimand that he was overreacting?

Amos didn't slow as he walked from the front door to the kitchen and back. Where were Linda and Polly?

They'd taken Leah's buggy this morning and left a note saying they were going shopping, but he hadn't seen them at the store. When he'd come home and found they were missing, too many unsettling scenarios raced through his head.

Perhaps Linda had regained her memories and was heading to the place she and the *kind* had been going before she was hurt. Could she have gotten tired of waiting for those memories to return and decided to try to find her way to her original destination on her own? Or maybe she'd bumped her head and couldn't remember him.

The last bothered him most. To imagine her forgetting him when he knew he'd never be able to forget her was painful.

Suddenly Amos heard buggy wheels crunching through the frozen slush on the lane. He sped out of the house and across the yard. He recognized the dark brown buggy horse. The buggy's wheels had barely stopped turning before he grabbed the door handle and threw it open.

"Where have you been?" He reached into the buggy and grasped Linda by the shoulders.

Startled by his vehemence, she jerked away from him. "Amos, have you lost your mind?"

"Almost." He drew back his hands when he saw Polly's face was as pale as Linda's. Frightening the *kind* because he'd been fearful they'd left forever was foolish. "Where have you been?"

"I left a note for Wanda." She motioned for Polly to climb out, then looked at him pointedly.

He stepped aside to give her room to step down. "I know you did. I read it."

"Then why are you asking where we were? It said we were going—?"

"Shopping, but you weren't at the store. I know. I checked every inch when Leah came to tell me you and Polly hadn't come home for lunch."

"Yours isn't the only store in the world, Amos Stoltzfus."

Her words were like a slap to the face of a hysterical person. It shocked him out of his foolish fear.

"You're right," he said. "But I thought you'd lost your purse along with your suitcase after you were injured at the bus station."

"I did, but Polly didn't lose the money I apparently gave her."

As she explained what the *kind* had told her, he waited for his heart to halt its frantic beat and return to its usual pace. He couldn't halt his fingers from curving around her shoulders, this time gently.

"Your note said you'd be back in a few hours," he said as he gazed into her amazing eyes shining in the light from the kitchen. "When you didn't return…"

"I wanted to surprise everyone with gifts on Christmas. I never guessed we'd be delayed by traffic and crowds."

"Where did you go?"

"To the Rockvale Outlet shops."

His hands tightened on her. He forced them to ease before he hurt her. "Did *you* lose your mind? Driving along that busy highway this close to Christmas?"

"When I saw the traffic whizzing by, I went to the

post office. A man there told me how to go through Gordonville and toward Bird-in-Hand before heading south on the farm roads."

"At least you were sensible about that." He put up his hand before she could retort. "I'm sorry, Linda. I keep saying the wrong thing, but I've got a *gut* excuse. I was worried about you and Polly. I had the craziest thoughts about you forgetting us."

She shivered. "Don't even think that."

"I try not to."

"Maybe I should wear the bike helmet all the time." Her attempt at a smile sent a pulse of delight through him. She was trying to make *him* feel better.

"Maybe you should."

As she urged Polly to let *Mamm* know she and Linda were home, he unhitched the horse.

"Do you need help with your packages?" he asked as he led the horse toward the barn.

"So you can find out what I bought?" She wagged a finger at him as if he were no older than the little girl. "I'll handle them on my own."

"You're a stubborn woman."

"*Ja*, I am." She smiled while matching his steps. "And you're a caring man. *Danki* for worrying about us."

He wasn't sure how to reply to her comment, so he didn't. He enjoyed bantering with her as they walked into the barn. He didn't know how much time they'd have together, and he intended to enjoy every moment and try not to fret about the unknowns. He'd leave the future in God's hands where it belonged and be grateful for the time he had with her…however much there was.

Chapter Seven

Easing around half-frozen puddles of slush in the parking lot the next day, Linda was grateful for the boots Amos had lent her. The snow had started melting yesterday but hardened into ice in the evening. During the night, she'd heard a plow going along the road at the end of the farm lane. It'd scraped on the asphalt and spread sand to keep the road safe for *Englisch* vehicles.

And for her. More than once on the walk from the farm, her foot had skidded on black ice she hadn't noticed. Probably because her thoughts were on her conversation with Amos yesterday. So many things she'd wanted to say when they stood face-to-face. So much of the moment she wanted to enfold in her heart and treasure it forever. The powerful emotions in Amos's eyes and the strong but gentle way he'd gripped her arms as he revealed how worried he'd been for her. She savored the memory of the husky warmth in his relieved voice.

She was silly to think about such things. Pulling her knitted scarf closer to her mouth, she pushed it aside when the fabric swiftly became damp and cold from her breath. She ducked her head into the biting wind as she stepped into the parking lot of the Stoltzfus Family Shops. Several buggies were parked in front of the shop on the far end from Amos's store. It belonged to his older brother Joshua who worked on buggies.

A wisp of smoke tainted the air. It must have come from the smithy behind the shops.

Hurrying as the wind picked up, Linda's foot slid again. She grabbed a nearby buggy.

"Careful there," she heard from her right. "Are you okay?"

She saw a familiar face behind a clumpy, pale blond beard. "I am, Isaiah."

He nodded. "You've got a *gut* mem…" He flushed, making his uneven beard stand out more on his face.

"It's all right," she hurried to say. "Please don't watch your words around me. If everyone does, I'm going to feel more lost. Amos suggested if I make myself comfortable here, my memories might return."

"He may be right. Amos thinks deeply about things."

"I've noticed he doesn't talk just to have something to say."

"Which makes him a *gut* source of advice." He grinned. "Don't tell him I said that. It doesn't do for a little brother to be complimented by his older brother." He grew serious. "I don't know if anyone told you that I haven't been a minister very long. I'm still wet behind the ears, as *Mamm* would say. However, if you want to talk to me at any time, I'm willing to listen."

Linda thanked him. The Stoltzfus family members

were eager to do whatever they could to help her live in this strange limbo.

"Reuben asked me," Isaiah said, "to let you know he's been contacting other plain communities, not just Amish ones. Because you weren't wearing a *kapp*, we can't be certain you're Amish."

"I didn't consider that." Everything about the Amish life seemed right to her, but other groups in addition to Old Order Amish like the Stoltzfus family had the same customs and plain clothing and spoke *Deitsch*. Wanting to change the subject, she asked, "Will you be coming to your *mamm*'s house for Christmas Day or will you spend it with your wife's family?"

"My wife died earlier this year," he said, his voice wavering.

She wished she could take the question back. "Oh, I'm sorry. I didn't know."

"There's no need to apologize. Rose's family misses her as I do, and I worry any time I visit, it's another reminder to them of what should have been."

"I doubt they forget it, whether you visit or not." She put her gloved hands over her mouth, horrified she'd spoken so bluntly.

Instead of a scowl or a sharp retort—both of which she deserved—Isaiah gave her a sad smile. "I understand why you and Amos get along well. He cuts to the heart of the truth, and so do you."

"Forgive me. I shouldn't have said that."

"No, it's okay. I know her family grieves for her, and I fear them seeing my sorrow makes them feel worse." He turned away. "Be careful where you walk. The ice is treacherous." He didn't give her a chance to answer before he walked toward his smithy.

Linda sighed into her scarf. She needed to be more like Amos and think before she spoke. Bending her head into the wind, she walked toward his store.

Help me, Lord, to say the right thing to these kind people who have taken me into their home. I don't want to burden them further.

She raised her head when a woman called a greeting to her. Linda waved, recognizing the woman she'd met on Sunday, but not sure of her name.

Going inside, Linda saw it was crowded with dozens of shoppers. Everyone waited as the person ahead of them in the aisle took what they needed off the shelf before they moved forward. Several women pushed shopping carts, but others carried plastic baskets.

She stepped forward when the door reopened and an elderly couple entered. Stretching, she picked up the last basket and handed it to them before slipping around the end of the aisle...and bumping into Amos. She was surprised he wasn't behind the counter taking care of his customers.

He juggled the cans he was carrying and managed not to drop any. Setting them in a cart behind her and nodding to the woman's thanks, he wiped his hands on the apron he wore over his light blue shirt and black trousers.

"Can I help you find something, Linda?" he asked as he smiled at two other customers who pushed between them.

"Busy day today, huh?"

He looked toward the cash register. "If Micah hadn't offered to help ring people up, it'd be even more chaotic. What do you need?"

She didn't give him the answer burning on her lips. That she needed his arms around her as she spilled the truth she wanted to give him her heart. "Two things. First, your *mamm* needs some Karo syrup. We're planning to make popcorn balls for the cookie exchange tomorrow."

His harried expression eased into a smile. "I hope you plan to keep a few at home for those of us with a sweet tooth."

"You'll have to wait and see. *Gut* things come to those who wait."

"I've told you before that I don't have a lot of patience."

"Then this is the perfect time to learn it."

He chuckled. "This way." He led her along the aisle. Plucking the plastic bottle from among other baking supplies, he handed it to her. "What's the other thing you're looking for?"

"Leah mentioned you sell fabric."

"*Ja.* My selection isn't big, but I try to keep a few bolts for those who don't want to drive to Intercourse."

"Would it be possible for me to work at the store in exchange for enough material to make a new dress for Polly? I'd like to work on it tonight and tomorrow night after she goes to bed, so she can have it Christmas morning."

He took her arm and steered her through the crowd gathered around the shelves. They went along another aisle leading toward the rear of the store. No other shoppers were there. He gestured toward a dozen bolts of cloth on the shelves behind the counter. "Take what you need."

"But I want to—"

"You don't have to work here. You're helping *Mamm* and Leah at home. That's payment enough for me."

"Amos—"

Again he interrupted her. "Haven't you heard it's better to give than receive, Linda? Let me give you a couple of yards of fabric for Polly's dress."

"Danki," she said, putting her hand on his arm. "This will mean so much to Polly. She's tried not to complain."

"She has had a *gut* role model in not complaining."

"Who?"

"You." He tapped her nose and chuckled. "You have more right than anyone I know to complain, but you don't."

"I do. All the time."

"Really? I don't remember hearing you."

She smiled. "Well, maybe not aloud, but inside my head there's a lot of whining going on."

"It must be noisy in there."

"You've got no idea." She lowered her eyes. "Amos, I've done a terrible thing."

"You?"

"I asked Isaiah about spending the holiday with his wife's family. I didn't know she'd died. I feel…"

Amos waited for her to finish. He hated to see Linda miserable. Was that what she was going to say? She felt miserable? Embarrassed? Sad? Knowing his brother must have reassured her, he wasn't sure what he could say to comfort her. He'd been fighting the yearning to take her into his arms and hold her close since Reuben had given her the bad news yesterday. He wanted to keep her from being battered more.

"I feel ashamed," she whispered.

"Ashamed?" he repeated, astonished. He hadn't imagined her saying that.

"*Ja.* I've been feeling sorry for myself because I can't remember my past, but your brother has lost so much more than memories. He's lost the woman he loves and his life with her." Tears she hadn't let fall before welled up in her eyes, teetered on her lashes, then tumbled down her cheeks. "How could I fail to see how blessed I've been that you and your family took us in? I may have lost my memories, but I've gained more with you."

What could he say? Any words he could think of seemed useless, but she was in pain.

He realized nobody else was in the back of the store. Knowing he was being bold, he splayed his fingers along her cheek and tipped her face so her gaze meshed with his. He could stand like this for the rest of his life.

No, he wanted more. He wanted to kiss her. When her eyes widened, he was certain her thoughts mirrored his. He started to bend toward her, but froze when he heard a guffaw behind him.

Larry Nissley grinned as he hefted his overstuffed shopping basket. It was filled with cheese. Despite his one-time crush on Leah, he didn't let Ezra winning her heart keep him from being a fan of Ezra's special cheeses.

"You've got a pretty assistant, Amos." Larry chuckled.

"I do." He winked at Linda who flushed.

"But you've always been one with an eye for a lovely lady, haven't you? Guess you didn't learn your lesson after Arlene dumped you. I'd heard you're courting another mysterious lady." He laughed as he turned to her. "What are you hiding from my buddy Amos? Hope it's not a boyfriend or two you've conveniently forgotten to mention."

Amos sensed rather than saw, because he was careful not to look in Linda's direction, her shock at what Larry said. She backed away and murmured something he couldn't discern before she rushed behind the counter. She grabbed a bolt of dark green cloth and fled with it.

"Did I say something wrong?" Larry asked.

"What do you think?" He left the man sputtering behind him as he went after Linda.

Why hadn't he guessed Larry could say something thoughtless? The man had a reputation for uttering the wrong thing at the worst time.

By the time Amos had made his way through the packed store, Linda was walking away along the road. Should he go after her? He never would have described his heart as careless, but he couldn't deny he'd been ignoring the truth. First, he'd fallen for Arlene Barkman's pretty face, not heeding his brothers' warnings she was playing him for a fool. He'd told himself everyone was due one mistake, and Arlene had been his.

But his heart did jumping jacks whenever Linda was near. For all he—and she—knew, she belonged to another man. He couldn't accuse her of leading him on, because she'd done nothing beyond the boundaries of friendship. Any betrayal was by his own thoughts as he wondered if her lips would be as sweet as her smile.

Should he let her go? No!

Amos called Linda's name and was relieved when she stopped. He caught up with her and said, "I owe you an apology."

"You don't owe me anything." She glanced at the cloth she carried. "I'd say the debt is mine."

"I should have told Larry to be quiet."

"You aren't to blame for what someone else says."

"But I'm to blame for knowing how he can be and not stopping him before he said something stupid."

She began walking again. "Don't worry about it, Amos. I know you need to get back to the store, and I want to hide this fabric so Polly doesn't guess what I'm doing. I'll see you at supper."

He couldn't let her walk away when Larry's words hung between them. "Linda, I need to be honest with you."

"Aren't you always?" She paused and faced him.

"*Ja*, except about one incident in my past."

"With Arlene?"

Amos nodded. "I should have told you before that Arlene Barkman and I walked out together for almost six months. Not many people knew, though my brothers suspected. Arlene wanted to keep our courting a big secret."

"Most couples keep quiet about walking out together."

"*Ja*, but they're seen leaving youth events together or caught flirting or talking to each other. Arlene insisted we be extra circumspect. She wouldn't let me take her home unless I left on my own and we met somewhere far from everyone else. She made it seem like a game, and it was, but not the one I thought we were playing. Fool that I was, I swallowed her unending excuses of why she couldn't take a ride with me some nights. I was like a trout on the line which she played with, but never reeled in."

"I don't understand. What game was she playing?"

"One I had no chance of winning." He met her eyes as he said, "I wasn't the only man who was hearing her excuses."

"She was being courted by another man at the same time?"

"Two others."

"Two?" she asked in disbelief. "She was walking out with three different men at the same time?"

"I believed her explanations while she strung me along. I couldn't imagine she wasn't being truthful. I even believed her when she publicly announced everything about me that she found fault with. At least, until her engagement to another man was published during a church Sunday service the morning after I'd taken her for a buggy ride."

Linda didn't speak for a long moment, and he wondered what she was thinking. That he was a besotted fool? That he couldn't be trusted to see the truth?

He'd misread her because, as she shifted the bolt in front of her to hold it with both arms, she asked, "How long ago did that happen?"

"Almost five years ago."

"And you haven't forgiven her?"

He laughed without humor. "Oh, I've forgiven her. It wasn't hard because I realized I didn't want a woman who'd lied from the beginning. I've had a harder time forgiving myself for such poor judgment."

"Each of us makes bad decisions sometimes, Amos." She put her hand on his arm. "I'm sure I've done stupid things. I wish I could remember them, so I could share them with you now."

"I wish you could, too. Not to make me feel better, but because you'd have your memories." He kicked a stone across the road. As it clattered on the asphalt, he said, "It's my turn to say I'm ashamed. No, let me finish," he added when she started to answer. "I've spent the past five years feeling sorry for myself. For so long I thought the best thing God could do was take away my memories of Arlene and my humiliation. I see how stupid that was because I'm watching you suffer from losing everything you knew. I'm ashamed I thought banishing memories was worth what it would cost me."

"It's okay." She put her gloved fingers on his arm, and he realized for the first time he'd left his coat in the store. He'd been determined to reach her and hadn't felt the cold.

Nor did he feel it now because from where her hand rested, a luscious warmth oozed through him, thawing the last of the ice clamped around his heart. But his breath froze in his chest when she spoke.

"When I remember what I've forgotten, Polly and I will have to leave. I don't want there to be any bad memories between us, Amos."

"You don't have to leave." The words escaped his lips before he could stop them; then he knew he didn't want to halt them.

"We must have at least one family waiting for us. Don't you think they've waited long enough for us to come to them?"

The words burned on the tip of his tongue. She could remain in Paradise Springs, and they could discover if the attraction between them could grow into love.

But as she turned and continued walking toward the farm, he didn't try to stop her. He couldn't, because he knew she was right. But knowing did nothing to relieve his sorrow at the thought of her leaving one day and never coming back.

Chapter Eight

The snow fell all through the night. It piled up around the house, blocking doors and clinging to windows in icy patterns.

Linda glanced through her bedroom window while she dressed in the dark on Christmas morning, grateful she didn't have to go outside. The snow swirled, and the barns were barely visible. She saw movement. Amos's younger twin brothers. Last night, they'd announced their Christmas gift to Ezra was to do his chores this morning to allow him the rare chance to sleep later than 4:00 a.m.

Before leaving the room, she adjusted the quilt over Polly. The little girl had been awake late last night, complaining of a tummy ache. Linda suspected Polly had snuck extra cookies at the exchange yesterday.

The propane lamp in the kitchen was glowing when she emerged from the *dawdi haus*. She wasted no time going to the refrigerator and getting what she needed to make breakfast. Soon the aroma of *kaffi* wafted through the kitchen, and she was putting cinnamon rolls into the oven.

"Smells *gut*" came a voice from behind her, the voice that released a thousand butterflies in her stomach.

"Frelicher Grischtdaag, Amos.*"* She closed the oven and straightened.

"Merry Christmas to you, too." He was barefoot as he entered the kitchen, and his hair was tousled as if he'd forgotten to comb it. She'd never seen him look so adorable. "I didn't expect to see you up this early."

"I overheard Micah and Daniel talking about their Christmas gift for Ezra, and I thought I'd offer the same to Leah." She began to break eggs into a bowl so she could scramble them. "She does a lot for us." She smiled. "I've offered to make breakfast every other day from now on."

"That's generous of you."

Her heart danced at his admiring tone, and she dared to believe the discomfort of yesterday at the store could be put behind them. She'd been surprised by his friend's words and saddened by how many years Amos had lived with the pain of betrayal.

But she didn't say that. If she chose the wrong words, she could make him feel worse, so instead she said, "You've been kind to Polly and me. Making breakfast is a small way to repay your kindness."

"Did you get Polly's gift finished?"

"Ja, except for the hem. I want to measure it on her. She's growing so fast."

"She's going to love it."

"I hope so." She poured milk in with the eggs and began to whip them.

"And what gift do you want most for Christmas?" he asked.

Linda put down the fork and faced him. "You know what I want most."

"To have your memories back?"

"Ja." She handed him a cup of *kaffi* before turning away. With her face averted, she said, "I can't stop thinking of the people wondering where Polly and I are. Her grandparents. The ones we were on our way to…for a visit? To stay? So many questions and too few answers."

"Have you noticed any change? Any faint glimpse of a memory?"

She shook her head.

"Nothing? Just emptiness?"

She stepped to the window. "Look at the storm."

"What am I supposed to see?"

"What do you see?"

"Snow blowing in every possible direction."

"And beyond the snow?"

He shrugged. "I know the barns and fences and trees are there, but I can't see them. Only snow."

"That's how it feels for me when I try to remember what my life was before I crossed the bridge. It's as if I stepped out of a blizzard in my mind. I know there are things on the other side of that bridge. Things that happened to me, experiences for more than two decades of my life. I know they're there. As you know the barns and fences and trees are there."

"But you can't see them." He sighed. "I think I'm beginning to understand for the first time all you've lost."

"I can't see my memories or hear them or feel them, but I know they're there." She turned to check the rolls in the oven. "Sit down, and I'll get your breakfast ready."

"No hurry. I'll wait until Micah and Daniel are back and *Mamm* is up."

Linda nodded. Christmas was meant to be spent with family. She thanked God that she had Polly and the Stoltzfus family with her to celebrate the day of Christ's birth.

As if she'd called the little girl, the door from the *dawdi haus* burst open, slamming against the wall. Polly ran in, sobbing so hard she teetered.

Linda went to her as Amos rose from the table. "*Liebling, was iss letz*? Are you hurt?"

Polly clung to her and wept. "I want my *grossmammi* and *grossdawdi*. You promised we'd see them on Christmas."

"I did?" She looked over the *kind*'s shuddering shoulders to Amos who regarded her sadly.

"*Ja.* You said we'd spend Christmas Day with them and *Grossmammi* would make chocolate pancakes."

She knelt by the little girl. Brushing damp hair from Polly's face, she said, "I'd give anything to keep that promise, Polly. I wish I could."

"You're mean! You don't want to share them with me."

Taken aback by the *kind*'s anger, she struggled for something to say. Amos stepped forward and held out his hand to Polly. The little girl put her much smaller one in his.

He sat at the table and lifted Polly to sit on one knee. "Do you believe Linda would lie to you?"

The little girl bowed her head, then shook it. "But she promised."

"And Linda always keeps her promises to you, doesn't she?"

Polly nodded.

"And Linda would keep this one if she could. Don't you think so?"

"Ja." The single word was reluctant. "But I want to see my *grossmammi* and my *grossdawdi*."

"You will. *I* promise that as Linda did."

Looking at him, she whispered, "But she didn't keep her promise."

"She will as soon as she can, and I'm going to help her keep that promise to you."

"Really?"

He gave her a grin and a wink. *"Ja,* I promise." His smile broadened when Polly flung her arms around him and squeezed him. *"Ach!* Don't keep me from breathing." Bouncing her on his knee, he added to Linda, "When will those eggs be ready for a hungry little girl?"

"As soon as she wants them…unless she'd rather have French toast," she replied, more grateful to Amos than she could put into words. As Polly cheered about the special treat, Linda smiled at the man holding the *kind*.

He started to smile but glanced at the door as his brothers entered along with a blast of cold air. Soon everyone was saying *"Frelicher Grischtdaag"* as she cooked French toast. Serving the first piece to Polly, Linda hoped the rest of the day would get better.

An hour later, after gifts had been shared, Polly tugged on Linda's hand. "Let's go and play in the snow!"

"It's chilly."

"I want to use my new mittens." She grabbed the bright blue ones Wanda had knit for her. They were a smaller version of the red mittens Wanda had given Linda.

"I'll take her," Amos said, standing from his chair near the fireplace. "I want to check the sleigh to make sure it's ready to take us visiting tomorrow for Second Christmas." He smiled at Polly. *"Komm.* Let's go."

Linda was about to speak when she realized, though he offered the little girl his hand, his gaze was focused on Linda. What she saw in his eyes was warm enough to melt the snow. He arched his brows in a clear challenge.

Putting down Polly's dress that she'd started hemming, Linda stood. "I'll go, too, to keep an eye on her."

"Bundle up," Wanda said, "and don't stay out too long. This is the coldest Christmas I remember in a long time."

Linda did that and made sure Polly's coat was buttoned to her chin before wrapping a thick scarf around her neck and over her stocking hat. Pulling wool pants on beneath the *kind*'s dress, she tucked them into Polly's boots.

She followed the little girl and Amos outside. Polly danced around in the new snow, her despair from before breakfast set aside. Not forgotten, Linda knew, because every once in a while she saw tears bubbling into the little girl's eyes.

"She's going to be fine," Amos said as he walked beside Linda through the snow that reached the top of her boots.

"I've been praying for that."

He stopped and faced her. The mist from their breaths combined and hung in the air between them, an outward sign of the connection growing between them. That connection had allowed her when she was in his arms to toss aside her brave facade and release the tears that had been strangling her. With Amos, she didn't have to be stoic. He never jumped to conclusions when she spoke of fears and hopes. Instead, he thought long and hard about what she'd said.

"Praying is the best thing you can do." He smiled at her. "*Danki* again for the box of highlighters you got for me."

"I thought they'd make the perfect gift for the next time you have to check off an invoice."

"*Ja*, perfect. If you were there using them."

She looked away from the potent emotions in his eyes. He shouldn't be looking at her like that, but she couldn't deny how special she felt when he did.

He picked up one end of her scarf and tickled her nose. "*Komm*, before your nose is as red as the cherries in *Mamm*'s pie."

When he turned to walk away, Linda checked what Polly was up to. The little girl had made a snow angel and was rolling snow to make a snowman. Linda bent to scoop up a handful. It compacted into a ball. Without warning Amos, she let it fly. The snow exploded on his barn coat.

He turned and laughed. "Why couldn't you have forgotten how to make a snowball?"

"What fun would that be?" She gathered another handful of snow and shaped it before aiming it at him.

With a playful growl, he strode toward her. He caught her wrist and shook the snowball from her hand. He held up a snowball of his own.

She tried to knock it away, but the deep snow caught her legs. She couldn't keep from shrieking as they fell together. Flakes flew everywhere as Polly ran to them. The little girl threw herself on top of them.

It took longer than Linda had expected to get untangled because the snow made it difficult to move. When Amos picked up Polly and put her on her feet, she ran toward the snowman she was making.

"I don't know about you," he said, "but sitting in this snow is a cold business."

"Ja." Linda drew her feet beneath her to stand. When she got up, she looked down at him. "Are you going to stay there?"

"I may if you threaten to pelt me with snowballs again."

She laughed. "I'll take pity on you, Amos. No more snowballs."

"Gut." He stood and wiped snow off his wool trousers. "It's cold."

"It is." She turned toward the barn. "Shall we get warmed up?"

"I thought you'd never ask." His voice took on a gentle huskiness that made her look over her shoulder in surprise. Amusement had vanished from his face as his gloved hands framed her face and tilted it toward him.

For a moment, she relished the sweetness of his touch, then she yanked herself away. What was she doing? If she was married… She put her hands to her heated face.

"Linda…" He didn't continue.

She wished he would because she didn't know what to say either. She couldn't tell him she didn't want him to touch her or kiss her. That would be lying. But there were too many things about herself she didn't know. Things that might mean she shouldn't be standing face-to-face with him.

"Linda," he began again. *"Ich liebe dich."*

"How can you say you love me when you don't know me?" She wrapped her arms around herself, wishing the arms were his.

"I know you, Linda."

"How can you know me when I don't know myself who I am? Who I *really* am?"

He put his hands on her arms, sliding them to cup her elbows. He didn't pull her closer as he bent so their eyes were level. "I know exactly who you are. You're a *wunderbaar* woman who cares about those around her."

"Am I? Am I *really*? What if I was different before and I can't remember?"

"What if you were?"

Her head jerked up at the question she hadn't expected him to ask. Maybe she should have, because Amos preferred the truth.

"Linda," he continued when she didn't answer, "you can always be the woman you are now, whether or not you regain your memories. God gave us free will to find ourselves and to choose whether we want to walk with Him or not. He loves us, no matter what we decide, though He must mourn when one of His *kinder* decides to turn away from Him. No matter what caused you to lose your memories, I believe it was part of His plan for your life. Not many of us get a chance to remake our lives. You have.

"How can you have been a horrible person?" He looked at where Polly was rolling a ball of snow as big as she was. "Every truth you need to know is in her eyes. Polly loves you with the simple trust of a *kind* who has never had a reason to question that trust. Think of what she's told you of the past you've shared. Of the stories you've read to her and the songs and games you've taught her. She hid money because you asked her to. She never questioned why you'd ask. She never questioned why you got off the bus in Paradise Springs that night. She trusts you. She *loves* you. Could she feel that way if you weren't a *gut* person?"

"Are you always wise?" She let her shoulders ease from the tension aching across them.

"Hardly. Otherwise, I would have been better prepared when you pelted me with snowballs."

She laughed, her dismay vanishing as if it'd never existed. The sound drifted away when his fingers brushed her cheek, sending music through her heart. As his mouth lowered toward hers, her eyes closed. He found her lips, and she leaned into his strength. As close as they stood, she was unsure if the shivers were hers or his or both. She slid her hands along the powerful muscles of his arms, and he enfolded her to him. His kiss offered everything she wanted. When he stroked her back, tingles raced along her spine.

He lifted his mouth far enough away to whisper, *"Ich liebe dich,* Lìnda.*"* His expression had become vulnerable and honest. "Do you love me, too?"

"Ja! Ich liebe dich." For a moment, joy soared through her, then she stepped away. Looking across the snow toward the barn, she said, "Falling in love with you should change everything, but it doesn't. Not when I don't know what life I had before I came here. I must know what my life was in the past before I can consider what my future should be. I shouldn't let you kiss me when I may be married."

"What if your memories never return?"

"I don't know." She doubted she'd ever spoken such hopeless words and she longed for him to say something to ease her desperation as he had before.

Instead he drew her into his arms and leaned her head against his chest. Hearing his heart thud beneath her ear, she knew the truth. For the first time, he didn't have an easy answer for her.

Or any answer at all.

When a knock came at the front door after Linda had excused herself to put Polly to bed, Amos frowned and looked at his brothers. Who was calling at such a late hour on Christmas? What visit couldn't wait until Second Christmas tomorrow?

To be honest, he wasn't in the mood to have company. He'd spent the day trying to pretend his dreams weren't being dashed into splinters again. But unlike when Arlene had dumped him, he had to see the pain on the face of the one he loved. Oh, Linda had done an excellent job of trying to hide her thoughts from everyone else, but his heart seemed linked to hers now, and he could sense her sorrow.

Amos was closest to the door, so he got up and went to open it. He didn't want to leave anyone standing out in the cold. Glancing out a window as he passed, he didn't see any lights in the yard, but *Englischers* often got lost on the country roads and stopped to ask for directions.

Lost… He understood that feeling. He'd believed if he ever found his way back to love, he'd have the certainty and reassurance he craved. Maybe he was a greater simpleton than he'd believed.

Opening the door, he stared. The people standing on the front porch weren't lost *Englischers* nor were they among the Stoltzfus family's neighbors. They were, however, plain in dress by what he could see beneath their dark wool coats. A man and a woman, at least a generation older than he was. Perhaps two.

"*Komm* in, *komm* in," he said when the old woman shivered.

Thanking him, they entered the house. He heard his brothers coming to their feet, as curious as he was.

"This is the Stoltzfus farm?" the old man asked as he unbuttoned his coat.

Amos nodded and glanced at Ezra who had come to stand beside him.

His older brother said, "I am Ezra Stoltzfus. This is my farm."

"I'm Norman Glick," the elderly man said. "This is my wife Yvonne."

"Take off your coats and get warm." Amos gestured toward the living room and the hearth.

As if Amos hadn't spoken, Norman went on, "I hope yours is the Stoltzfus farm we've been looking for. We're searching for our two missing *kins-kinder.* Our two granddaughters who were traveling from Millersburg, Ohio. They were supposed to arrive almost two weeks ago, but they never did. We and our son and his wife and family have been looking for them everywhere between here and Millersburg, but we ran into blank walls." He glanced at his wife, then hurried on. "That is, until we heard from our bishop that two girls had found their way to a Stoltzfus farm in this part of Lancaster County. We came as quickly as we could to discover if they were *our* girls."

Amos didn't hesitate. As shock paralyzed his brothers, he crossed the kitchen in a few long steps. The door to the *dawdi haus* was ajar. He yanked it aside and rushed inside. Hearing Linda's lyrical voice reading a story to Polly, he burst into the bedroom.

"Amos!" Shock brightened Linda's eyes. "Is everything okay?"

"Maybe better than okay." He grabbed her arm, plucked the storybook from her hand and pulled her to her feet. He motioned for Polly to follow as he tugged

Linda from the room. "An older couple has just arrived. They're looking for their lost granddaughters. You and Polly!"

Linda tried to get her mind around what Amos was saying. Someone had come seeking her and Polly? She stared at him. "But I thought—"

"That you'd recover your memories and go looking for them?" He smiled as he lifted Polly and settled her on his shoulders. "What does it matter? *Komm!* They're waiting to see you."

How could she explain what she didn't understand? Since she'd stumbled into the parking lot at the shops, she'd believed her memories would return to her at any moment. Then *she'd* find the answers to the puzzles taunting her.

Now...

Forgive me, Lord, for questioning Your way. I should be grateful if these people know Polly and me. But You know my heart and how happiness and hope can live side by side with grief at the idea of leaving here.

Lifting her chin so nobody could guess the disparity between what she felt and what she should be experiencing, she went with Amos. A single glance at him told her, even if she could conceal the truth from others, he knew what was in her heart. She treasured that realization.

They went into the kitchen. In the front room, she could see Amos's brothers as well as Wanda and Leah.

Polly wiggled to get down. The moment Amos set her on the floor, she ran and threw herself into the old woman's outstretched arms. *"Grossmammi! Gross-dawdi!"* The little girl sobbed with joy when the elderly man put his arms around her. Then Polly ran back to Linda and hugged her. "You kept your promise. Just as Amos said you would."

Everyone looked at Linda. On wooden feet that seemed to be trying to grow roots into the floor, she forced herself to move forward as the little girl ran back to her grandparents. Polly knew the couple, but Linda couldn't recall ever seeing them before. There was something about the shape of the old man's face that reminded her of Polly's, and the old woman had light blue eyes with navy edging them as Linda did.

The woman gasped, "It's you, Belinda! You're safe."

"My name is Belinda?" She'd hoped her name would feel comfortable on her lips and open her sealed memories so they could spill out, but the name was as unknown to her as the elderly couple.

"Ja." The old woman glanced from her to the others. "Why does she sound surprised at her own name?"

As Amos gave an abbreviated explanation, Linda learned the older couple's names. They were her grandparents, and Polly was her little sister. Their parents lived in Ohio, and she and Polly had come to Pennsylvania to spend the holidays with their grandparents who lived near Shippensburg, a long day's buggy ride to the west.

It made sense, and Polly knew the couple. It must be true, but...

"I'm sorry," Linda said as the Glicks looked at her with the hope she'd hug them as Polly had. "I don't know you. I can't—" Her voice broke as she thought of leaving the Stoltzfus family who had become *her* family and going with people who were strangers.

Yvonne smiled. "My dear *kind*, it doesn't matter if you don't remember us. We know you!"

When she held out her arms to her, Linda—she needed to think of herself as Belinda—embraced the old woman. Some sense having nothing to do with her brain but everything to do with heart recognized the hug's warmth.

"You're my *grossmammi*." It wasn't a question. It was a fact. As if someone flipped the pages of a book in her mind, her head was flooded with images. Not images, memories. Her memories! Not just the ones she'd made since she arrived in Paradise Springs, but an explosion of memories from her past. *Gut* ones of being with her family, including her little sister Polly…and her other five sisters and three brothers. Happy ones of friends and the other families in their district in Ohio. Sad ones of the passing of her other grandparents as well as the end of a relationship she'd started because she knew her family expected her to find a young man to marry. Because being with him had been wrong from the beginning, her heart had filled with guilt and sorrow for being less than honest with him.

And bad memories, including a very, very bad memory at a bus station on their way to Shippensburg. Pain thundered across her skull as it had when she'd been attacked and robbed when she went to find out about which bus she and Polly should take next. She'd left her little sister sitting in the waiting area, because she'd planned to go only as far as the ticket counter, which was right in plain sight. She hadn't even seen the ragged man approaching until he pressed his sharp knife against her side as he forced her around a corner. He stole her purse and struck her in the head with the knife's butt, leaving her forgetting even her own name.

Later, when Polly wasn't there to hear, she'd tell her family and Amos and his family the awful thing that had happened to her. For now, she silently thanked God for watching over her in that dark moment and guiding her to Amos.

Tears glistened in the eyes like her own. "*Ja*, I am your *grossmammi*. Thank the *gut* Lord that He restored your memories." Her *grossmammi* hugged her again before stepping back so she could be enfolded in her *grossdawdi*'s arms.

Dozens of questions were fired at her, too many for her to answer at once. She tried to explain, skirting what had happened at the bus station.

When she finished, from behind her, Amos cleared his throat. "May I ask you a question, Norman?"

"Ask anything, my boy," the old man said with a grin so wide it pushed his wrinkles to the edges of his cheeks. "You saved the lives of our *kins-kinder*. It's something we'll never forget."

"Is Linda—Belinda, I mean—married?"

She blushed at the smiles on his brothers' and *mamm*'s faces.

Norman replied, "No."

"Or walking out with anyone?" Amos asked.

The older couple glanced at each other and laughed

before Yvonne said, "The truth is, and Belinda didn't know anything about this, her parents sent her and Polly to us for the holiday in the hope she'd meet someone here who'd touch her heart as no one in Ohio had. From your grin, young man, I'd say their hopes have been fulfilled."

When Amos grasped her hand, Belinda let him tug her into the kitchen. In the front room, everyone else acted as if they were interested in the minuscule details of the Glicks' journey from Shippensburg. Their voices faded beneath her thundering heartbeat when Amos turned her to face him.

She gazed into his eyes, seeing the love that thrilled her heart. "My name is Belinda Glick. I know that is my real name. It is such a joy to know that."

"Then let me say this the right way. *Ich liebe dich*, Belinda." His fingers curved along her face, gentle, questing, joining their hearts together in the moment they'd longed for.

"I love you, too. My name may have changed, but my love for you hasn't."

He kissed her left cheek and murmured, "I can kiss you without guilt because I know you aren't walking out with anyone else." He brushed his lips on her right cheek. "And I can kiss you without remorse because you aren't married to someone else." Cupping her chin, he held her gaze. "There's one more way I want to kiss you. When you're my wife. Will you marry me?"

"*Ja*, I'll marry you."

His eyes twinkled as he pulled her against his broad

chest. "I know a marriage proposal may not be as *wunderbaar* a gift as a box of highlighters, but—"

She laughed and wrapped her arms around his shoulders. "Being married to you'll be the highlight of my life."

Snorting, he teased, "Because until a few moments ago, you couldn't remember most of your life, I don't know if that's a compliment or an insult."

"But I have all my memories now, and I still say being married to you will be the highlight of my life." She stilled his laughter and hers as she kissed him. Life with Amos would never be serious or boring. They'd make many memories together in the years to come, but one she'd always hold dear. As dear as she did this beloved man. It was this Christmas that she'd never forget.

* * * * *

Dear Reader,

We are an accumulation of our experiences. Sifting through memories can be our own version of *This is Your Life*. If those memories vanish, the question of "Who am I?" demands an answer. I know that, too well, in the wake of a head injury. Even now, almost twenty years later, I have no memories of the week before and the six months following the accident. I was strengthened and reassured by the love of my husband and family, who helped me see that the memories yet to be made were more important than the ones forgotten. It's a lesson I've kept close to my heart since. I hope you make some wonderful memories this holiday season.

Stop in and visit me at www.joannbrownbooks.com. Look for my next story in the Amish Hearts series coming soon from Love Inspired.

Wishing you many blessings,
Jo Ann Brown

THE NANNY'S TEXAS CHRISTMAS
Lone Star Cowboy League: Boys Ranch
by Lee Tobin McClain

When she agrees to be little Logan's nanny over the holidays, teacher Lana Alvarez never imagined she'd start falling for his handsome single dad. Now it's up to rancher Flint Rawlings and his son to convince cautious Lana that she's on their Christmas list.

MISTLETOE DADDY
Cowboy Country • by Deb Kastner

Returning to her hometown pregnant and alone, Vivian Grainger is surprised by the feelings she's developing for the gruff cowboy she's enlisted to help build her new business. Nick McKenna's never been attracted to bubbly blondes, but this Christmas he's finding himself wanting to make Viv and her baby his family.

HER CHRISTMAS FAMILY WISH
Wranglers Ranch • by Lois Richer

Ellie Grant has signed on as Wranglers Ranch camp nurse to provide a fresh start for herself and her daughter. But darling Gracie wants a daddy for Christmas, and she's set on persuading Ellie that widowed dad Wyatt Wright is exactly what they both need for their happily-ever-after.

AN ASPEN CREEK CHRISTMAS
Aspen Creek Crossroads • by Roxanne Rustand

All Hannah Dorchester wants is to give her orphaned niece and nephew a happy Christmas. But when the children's uncle—her ex-fiancé—returns seeking custody, can they come to an agreement—and maybe even find love again?

REUNITED AT CHRISTMAS
Alaskan Grooms • by Belle Calhoune

Dr. Liam Prescott is shocked to learn his wife, Ruby, survived the avalanche he thought had killed her, but has lived with amnesia the past two years. With Christmas fast approaching, can he help her remember why she fell in love with him in the first place?

YULETIDE REDEMPTION
by Jill Kemerer

This Christmas, Celeste Monroe is starting over with her baby nephew by moving in next door to Sam Sheffield. As they help each other overcome their scarred pasts and find peace, can they also create a family—together?

SPECIAL EXCERPT FROM

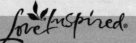

Could a Christmastime nanny position for the ranch foreman's son turn into a full-time new family for one Texas teacher?

Read on for a sneak preview of the third book in the **LONE STAR COWBOY LEAGUE: BOYS RANCH** *miniseries,* **THE NANNY'S TEXAS CHRISTMAS** *by Lee Tobin McClain.*

"Am I in trouble?" Logan asked, sniffling.

How did you discipline a kid when his whole life had just flashed before your eyes? Flint schooled his features into firmness. "One thing's for sure, tractors are going to be off-limits for a long time."

Logan just buried his head in Flint's shoulder.

As they all started walking again, Flint felt that delicate hand on his arm once more.

"You doing okay?" Lana Alvarez asked.

He shook his head. "I just got a few more gray hairs. I should've been watching him better."

"Maybe so," Marnie said. "But you can't, not with all the work you have at the ranch. So I think we can all agree—you need a babysitter for Logan." She stepped in front of Lana and Flint, causing them both to stop. "And the right person to do it is here. Miss Lana Alvarez."

"Oh, Flint doesn't want—"

"You've got time after school. And a Christmas vacation coming up." Marnie crossed her arms, looking determined. "Logan already loves you. You could help to keep him safe and happy."

Flint's desire to keep Lana at a distance tried to raise its head, but his worry about his son, his gratitude about Logan's safety, and the sheer terror he'd just been through, put his own concerns into perspective.

Logan took priority. And if Lana would agree to be Logan's nanny on a temporary basis, that would be best for Logan.

And Flint would tolerate her nearness. Somehow.

"Can she, Daddy?" Logan asked, his face eager.

He turned to Lana, who looked like she was facing a firing squad. "Can you?" he asked her.

"Please, Miss Alvarez?" Logan chimed in.

Lana drew in a breath and studied them both, and Flint could almost see the wheels turning in her brain.

He could see mixed feelings on her face, too. Fondness for Logan. Mistrust of Flint himself.

Maybe a little bit of… What was that hint of pain that wrinkled her forehead and darkened her eyes?

Flint felt like he was holding his breath.

Finally, Lana gave a definitive nod. "All right," she said. "We can try it. But I'm going to have some very definite rules for you, young man." She looked at Logan with mock sternness.

As they started walking toward the house again, Lana gave Flint a cool stare that made him think she might have some definite rules for him, too.

Don't miss
THE NANNY'S TEXAS CHRISTMAS
by Lee Tobin McClain, available December 2016
wherever Love Inspired® books and ebooks are sold.

www.LoveInspired.com

LIEXP1116